a Bed of Nails

Ron Tanner is fabulously imaginative, experimental, witty, often breathtaking. The series of "Revolutionary Militia" stories that thread the collection, and which are not science fiction so much as eco-fiction, have an eerie convincingness. Both male and female voices are handled beautifully although the prose is what we've come to call "muscular." At first I felt that this was actually two collections, one concerned with life as we know it and one as we fear it will be—but came to believe that the worlds are perfectly married through their askew inventiveness and their witty contemporary language. It's very assured and audacious work.

—Janet Burroway
  Final Judge, G.S. Chandra Prize for Short Fiction

a Bed of Nails

stories by

ron tanner

Winner of the
G.S. Sharat Chandra Prize for Short Fiction
Selected by Janet Burroway

BkMk Press
University of Missouri-Kansas City

BkMk Press
University of Missouri-Kansas City
5101 Rockhill Road
Kansas City, MO 64110
(816) 235-2558 (Voice)
(816) 235-2611 (Fax)
bkmk@umkc.edu
http://www.umkc.edu/bkmk/

Cover design: Jennifer Stutsman
Author Photo: Jill Eicher
Book interior design: Susan L. Schurman
Managing Editor: Ben Furnish
Editorial Consultants: Emily Iorg, Bill Beeson
Thanks to
Dennis Conrow, Ryan Cunningham, Sandra Davies,
Deron Denton, Jessica Hylan, Ashley Kaine, Michael
Nelson, Tim Pingelton, Tyler Ritter, Paul Tosh

Library of Congress Cataloging-in-Publication Data
Tanner, Ron, 1953-
     A bed of nails: stories / Ron Tanner.
          p. cm.
"Winner of the G. S. Sharat Chandra Prize for Short
Fiction selected by Janet Burroway."
     ISBN 1-886157-42-1 (alk. paper)
1. United States–Social life and customs–Fiction. 2. Balti-
more (Md.)–Fiction. 3. Science fiction, American. I. Title.
     PS3620.A69B44   2003
     813'.6–dc21
                                   2003011855

–acknowledgements–

New Letters: "A Bed of Nails"
Literary Review: "A Handful of Nails"
Turnstile: "Still Life"
The Iowa Review: "Garbage"
Indiana Review: "A Model Family"
Writers' Forum: "Loaves and Fishes"
Quarry West: "Ruth"
Michigan Quarterly Review: "The Ape in Me"
The Quarterly: "High Heat for Cotton"
Mid-American Review: "You're a Sergeant"
Chariton Review: "Telephone: an Act in Three Plays"
The Iowa Review: "Red Shoes"
The Massachusetts Review.: "The Day His Wife's Face Froze"

I wish to thank the following for their generous support in the writing of this collection: James A. Michner and the Copernicus Society of America, the Corporation of Yaddo, the Millay Colony for the Arts, and the Center for the Humanities at Loyola College, Maryland.

To Mrs. Ruth McClaren and Max Steele, teachers who made a difference.

~contents~

Grief may be joy misunderstood.

—Elizabeth Barrett Browning

a Bed of Nails

As Cooper glued brass fishhooks to a black and white photograph of a long-dead movie star, he watched Sarah at her desk in the adjoining room: she was writing again, editing copy from work or scribbling a note to herself. Framed by the bedroom doorway, she sat in profile, the desk lamp so bright behind her that it illuminated, through the wispy strays of her hair, an auburn aureole—the kind of crowning glow which, in paintings, Cooper had always dismissed as artistic hyperbole.

Nowadays, it seemed, he was always watching Sarah, as if she might do something remarkable or dreadful. Whenever she caught him watching her, she smiled her crooked smile, half her face frozen by Bell's palsy. Then he'd feel his own face pull in one direction like hers, a sympathetic reaction.

The neurologist said that, if "fortunate," she would recover full use of her face. Every morning after waking, every evening before sleeping, Sarah stood at the bathroom mirror and tested herself, attempting to work her mouth, raise her eyebrows, make simple expressions she had once taken for granted. The longer the paralysis remained, the less chance for recovery. "Or so we believe," the neurologist had said with a shrug.

The HMO doctors now believed Sarah had cancer. "It could be sarcoidosis," the GP had told her, "but that's rare, and even rarer when it occurs on only one side of the chest." Something had shown up on Sarah's chest x-ray. A black smudge in a white maze of bone.

The GP, a placid young woman who carried her stethoscope neatly looped always from the left pocket of her well-pressed lab coat, suggested Hodgkin's disease. So Cooper and Sarah had been through The Merck Manual of Diagnosis and Therapy many times, reading of the possibilities as if there might be a choice, a lesser evil.

Too often lately Cooper had pictured how Sarah might look a year from now, death camp thin, her sunken eyes bright with the knowledge of pain. Already she was twenty-three pounds underweight and so weak she could not walk a city block without losing her breath.

"What's the matter?"

Startled, he looked up and saw Sarah staring at him from across the room. He realized that she'd been watching him just as he'd been watching her. Synchronicity. He felt a smile rising but could not hold it, like wet clay slipping from his grasp.

"I don't know what to do with this." He nodded at the fishhooked photo. A lie. He knew exactly what to do. Make pain.

"That's never stopped you before." Now she smiled.

He felt acid rise in his throat, his eyes smarting.

"It's a joke, Matt. Lighten up."

He mustered a damaged smile finally. "Maybe you can help."

Another lie. It used to be that he'd sit at his table with only the vaguest notions, his found materials scattered before him like puzzle pieces. Sarah would give him direction—she'd always had a firmer sense of things to come. It was she who had told him to make mushrooms of the fluted lighting cowls he'd found last year; this was all he had needed, a simple suggestion to get him started. Still, he had doubted himself. Although he was a good craftsman, good at the technicalities, it seemed to him that his work, taken as a whole, articulated nothing in particular—there was no center of gravity, no unifying theme.

He'd felt this most stingingly last year when he'd gone to a show by a better-known, and younger, artist whom an influential critic had called "the most passionate, articulate sculptor of found art in America today." Every piece in this sculptor's show was a rendering of the leg he had lost in a boating accident the previous summer.

Talk about unity. Talk about theme.

Cooper had thought the show ridiculous but he couldn't deny that it *worked*, and he had begun to believe that he'd do better himself if he suffered a similar loss.

This had been only a passing thought, he reminded himself, never a wish.

"Matt, the fishhooks—they're a wonderful touch."

Sarah stood behind him now.

He felt his face flush with gratitude.

Fishhooks were streaming like tears from the eyes of the woman in the photograph.

"I'm thinking of calling it *Patient*," he said. "As in medical patient."

Sarah looked at him abruptly, as if to catch him smirking. He couldn't have been more serious.

When she continued to regard his face, searching for meaning he may have hidden there, he said, "You don't mind, do you?"

"The only thing I mind is that you don't really need my help." She glanced with regret at his work. It was another loss: she grew weaker while he grew stronger.

"This is hardly larger than a walk-in closet." Peggy, Sarah's mother, raised the blinds of the hospital room's one window and suddenly the wall behind the bed was orange with late afternoon light.

Cooper sat in the room's only chair. Then he stood abruptly. "They said twenty minutes, right?"

"That's doctor time, remember. A very elastic concept." She offered him a reassuring smile. He saw much of Sarah in her face: her green eyes, her thin nose, her expressive brows.

Peggy's arrival today had been a surprise. Family on both sides lived so far away, Cooper and Sarah had told everyone to stay home. The biopsy would be, after all, a routine procedure, a simple incision at the collarbone, then the insertion of a probe along the trachea. Within a year or so the scar would be nearly imperceptible. A year.

When Cooper took Peggy back to surprise Sarah in pre-op, Sarah had started sobbing, out of gratitude or relief or fear, it was hard to tell which. Too self-conscious, Cooper felt he was part of a made-for-TV melodrama. There were the kindly nurses looking on, the good mother holding her daughter—and he played the dutiful husband, standing stoically to one side, petting his wife's hand, saying, "Hey now, hey now...."

But this had been easier than it might have been. The irony of their ordeal these many months was that it had prepared them well for the worst. Five months ago, when the HMO had been confounded by Sarah's complaints, the GP said with finality that "It's either some type of allergy or it's AIDS." She had Sarah tested for HIV that afternoon, and that night Sarah and Cooper had huddled on their couch and wept. They spent the next six days trying to imagine how they would tell their families, their friends, their coworkers, determining who would take it badly—who might ostracize them—and who might take it well.

When the test came back negative, Cooper drove to the HMO clinic in a rage. Ignoring the receptionist, then the nurse's aide, then one, two, three nurses, all of them trying to make Cooper wait till the doctor could see him— "You don't have an appointment," one of them called after him—Cooper strode down the too-white corridor, which reeked of isopropyl alcohol, and, still followed by the nurses, he found the GP filling out a form in her cubicle. "What kind of doctor are you, that you can tell my wife she's got allergies *or* AIDS?" he said. "What kind of doctor are you that you can send her home after giving her an AIDS test without a single word of comfort or kindness? Do you have any idea what you've put her through?"

Bland-faced, the doctor nodded politely, pencil in hand, which hadn't moved from the form she was completing. It was then that Cooper realized the depth of his fear, realized that the HMO might let Sarah die because the GP was incompetent.

"It's a goddamn accident," Cooper blurted.

"Beg your pardon?"

He saw that he had startled Peggy. "A whim of nature," he said. "That's all this comes to."

She was sitting on the bed, staring at him earnestly, the way she must have stared so many times at Sarah when she was stubborn. "You'd rather it wasn't an accident?"

"You mean I get a choice?"

"The way you met Sarah, that was an accident, Cooper. The way you find art in garbage—tell me that isn't an accident."

"It isn't the same," he said. "We're dealing with damage here."

"I thought I was damaged when I was pregnant with Sarah," she said quietly. "That was an accident—it was devastating; I thought it would ruin my life."

He was stunned to hear this. He said, "Sarah never told me."

"Sarah doesn't know." Her eyes strayed from his. For a moment she watched her hand as it smoothed the sheet beside her. Then she said, in nearly a whisper, "It would be terribly ironic if I lost her as arbitrarily as I got her, don't you think?"

Cooper nodded in agreement, unable to speak.

The next morning, he visited Sarah. "You look well," he said. Like saying good morning, it came automatically.

"Fuck you," she said hoarsely.

A joke. But he knew she half meant it. "Well" must have sounded like a foreign country she'd never see except in sumptuous coffee-table books, a place of strong light and thin, bracing air.

"Glad to see you're in the fighting spirit," he said. He sat on the bed, took her hand, and tried not to stare at the IV leaking into her arm. She was slumped against a couple of pillows. Just above her collarbone was a single, finger-sized adhesive bandage where they had made the incision.

"You wouldn't believe how stoned I am," she said.

"Sure I would," he said, "you can hardly talk." She sounded like a stroke victim.

She nodded yes. Then she was asleep so suddenly it scared him. He debated whether or not to wait, but it seemed obvious that she'd be gone for a while. Such deep sleep. Before leaving, he turned on the TV because she liked hearing voices when she woke.

Peggy had coffee waiting for Cooper when he returned to the apartment. She handed him a cup, with sugar, no milk, the way he liked it. But she offered no smile. Worried about Sarah, he supposed. "She's sleeping," he told her.

Peggy nodded glumly. He noticed that her hand trembled ever so slightly when she raised her mug for a sip. She was wearing jeans and a gray sweatshirt, the sleeves pushed up to the elbows, the way Sarah wore hers. *This is how Sarah will look in thirty-four years,* he thought. It was a prediction whose certainty felt, for the moment, unassailable, as though Peggy had reserved her daughter's place in time.

"You got a phone call," Peggy said.

The hospital couldn't have called so soon. He had just left Sarah sleeping, with the TV on, the ward quiet, the nurses going about their business. The hospital wouldn't have called. Not yet. He looked to the phone, the innocuous white plastic cradle on the credenza. Lately his anticipation of the thing's chirping had made him jumpy and irritable. This birdlike noise, he thought ruefully, this is the sound of doom, arriving when you least expect it and sounding as you would never have imagined.

Peggy must have read the alarm in his face because

she added quickly, "It wasn't the hospital; it was the gallery you sent your slides to."

The mention of the gallery gave him a start. "My slides," he echoed. "The gallery called about my work?"

"The dealer was thrilled." She said this without enthusiasm. Cooper watched her walk to the window, where she lit a cigarette—usually she'd have asked him if he minded. She was staring out the window, at the brick wall across the alley. Taking her time. Why so pensive?

Peggy herself was a professional photographer. She should have been pleased for him.

"He said he thinks you've captured something," she continued, letting the smoke drift from her mouth as she spoke. "Something about illness and 'the inevitable.'" Her voice broke on "inevitable."

"He wants to know if you have more on the same theme." She was either nearly tearful or very angry, he couldn't tell which. "I think he's convinced that you or Sarah or both of you have AIDS. I think he's eager to cash in, Cooper."

"Cash in," how ugly that sounded.

At last she turned to him, arms crossed, her cigarette scissored between two fingers. The smoke made her squint. "You can't put your wife, my daughter, on display."

It wasn't a demand; it was a statement of disbelief, a quiet rebuke.

"It's not about Sarah," he said. "It's not personal that way."

"What if Sarah is dying?" she said. Her neck was flushed like Sarah's when Sarah was angry. "What if she's undergoing chemotherapy when your show opens? How will you feel about letting people buy pieces of her and tote them off to hang in their offices, their lobbies, their dens?"

He thought of pain as hard and sharp as fishhooks, of something that snags and won't let go.

Sarah was in her sit-up position, the bed adjusted to

an elongated "N".   Waif-like in her oversized gown, she seemed to be shrinking, the bed swallowing her.

"Bring me a present?" she called to Cooper as he entered the room, which smelled of Peggy's lilac perfume and faintly of ammonia.

"Missed you too," he said, relieved to see her awake and ready to joke.

Peggy nodded to him in greeting. Her "street" camera was slung from one shoulder. A Nikon nearly as old as he. *Oh, Jesus, Peggy, you'll take her photo yet, you'll put her in a show of your own—you won't be able to help it. Some suggestion of Sarah at least, in the photo of an empty bed, a hospital corridor, or a summer blouse hanging from a doorknob. And it won't be morbidity or self-indulgence that will compel you, it will be necessity, a matter of setting things right, of saying to the world, "This is how it was when I thought I'd lose my daughter."*

When Cooper saw Sarah's lunch on the bedside tray, Jell-O again, chicken broth, and ice cream, he knew he'd made a mistake. He had brought her two glazed donuts. Her favorites, but of course she couldn't eat them. It announced how little he was thinking of specifics nowadays, how too much was eluding his understanding.

"What's this?" She swiped playfully at the small paper bag he carried.   He stirred himself to make the best of it. "Forbidden fruit," he said. He let her take the bag, which she opened eagerly. Her lips were red from the cherry Jell-O, he noticed. It made her look girlish.

There was nothing to say. He and Peggy stood there, eyes fixed on that donut, the room quiet but for the murmur of the TV hanging from the opposite wall—a talk show, where a group of women were discussing a problem that had made one of them weep.

The phone rang. Cooper answered it. Sarah watched him, her brows arched wryly as if to say, So? Like waiting for a punch line. He felt his face forcing a smile. The image of a dead swallow entombed in an outsized syringe came to mind—one of his works from the show.

He heard Dr. Crockett, the surgeon, at the other end, a small, well-measured voice. The doctor said, "This looks like cancer, I'm sorry to say."

Just like that—cancer—and everything changed.

Cooper was surprised not by the relief he felt now that he and Sarah had an answer at last, but by the immediate realignment of his every thought towards the notion of treatment and cure. Instead of panic, there was mobilization, a great movement within him—he felt himself building walls, sending sentries to every tower, schooling his mind in the art of siege.

Sarah was still watching him, waiting for the word. Was it cruel to withhold from her for these few minutes while the doctor continued talking? Surely she saw the bad news in his face. She must have known that he'd have blurted the doctor's report immediately had it been good. But she remained stoic, though her solemn expression, her tightly compressed lips, her narrowed eyes, even the way she held that donut—like some odorous thing she needed to toss—all of this betrayed her.

"Oh, God," Peggy was saying, "oh, God."

She was sitting on the bed, watching too, as short of breath as Sarah after climbing a flight of stairs.

"This isn't fair," she continued, tears streaming down her cheeks. "This—"

"Shush," Sarah told her. "We haven't even heard the results."

Nothing had prepared Cooper for this, having to tell his wife and her mother that their day had turned to night, that if Sarah's treatment went well—the doctor conjectured that she was at stage 2-E of Hodgkin's disease, whatever that meant—she might live for another ten years.

Ten years.

Cooper held her hand as he told her. She was staring at the back of her mother's head, Peggy's face buried in Sarah's shoulder. Her mother's muffled weeping sounded like coughing from the next room.

"We're going to do everything," Cooper said, but

then stopped short, too aware of the appropriate things to say, all of them empty. He lay his head against Sarah's other shoulder to comfort her but it was she who comforted him, stroking his cheek with one finger. How must they have looked, the three of them huddled on the bed like that? Like the survivors of some distant war he'd see on the evening news now and then, a stunned family gathered in a basement archway shortly after a bombing.

Upon his return from his gallery opening two months later, Cooper was surprised at how good he could feel. The crunch of gravel under his wheels, the spots of light his car threw against the brick wall of his apartment building, the cool autumn breeze that swept past him as he coasted to a stop, the satisfying sound of closure when he slammed the car door—it all felt too good. His success, his head-swimming gratitude for the clamorous attention his work had brought him in a single night's showing, should have been tainted thoroughly by the dreadful prospect Sarah faced. It seemed terribly ironic that now, at his highest point, she would be at her lowest—so weak from chemotherapy that she could not attend the opening, could not even walk the three flights to their apartment without assistance. He stared up at the lighted windows of their one-bedroom, the fire escape looking like the zigzag of a fissure down the back of the building, and asked himself would he have exchanged his success for her good health?

If only it were that easy.

As he took the creaky, carpeted stairs two at a time, he rehearsed the many ways he might describe his opening. It seemed best to go slowly, to let her ease into it as she might have eased into a hot bath. But the moment he opened the apartment door and, from that distance, saw her push herself with difficulty to a sitting position in the bed, where she was surrounded by pillows, her books stacked on the nightstand and the TV on for company, he called with jubilation, "Tell me where you want to go, anywhere you want to go, and I'll take you—I've sold half the show already. Half the show!"

He saw her smile. And there it was—a complete expression, still a novelty six weeks after the Bell's had left her as mysteriously as it had arrived. A small blessing.

Since she'd started chemotherapy, Cooper was never quite prepared for her appearance after he'd been away from her for a few hours—it continued to unsettle him, how high her forehead was, how large her teeth looked, how her skin was bluish-gray and as dry as a November leaf, how her eyes seemed no brighter than candle flames he might have seen in a distant window. He was negotiating, he realized, the transition between Then and Now.

"You get used to anything if it becomes the norm, don't you?" she'd said to him recently.

He sat beside her on the mattress edge, took her hand in his. "Buyers," she said eagerly. "We've dreamed of this."

"I met a critic who said he was 'favorably impressed,'" he said.

"Send the review to my mother."

"That's cruel." But he laughed.

Sarah had caught on that her mother disapproved, and a few days ago had told him, "Don't let her intimidate you with guilt. My health and your show are completely separate."

Before making his installation, he had shown Sarah slides of his series and described each so that she'd know exactly what it meant to him: *that one I did the morning you couldn't pucker well enough to put on lipstick—you remember how we tried to laugh about it? this one I did the night you couldn't keep warm and I had to run hot baths for you—how many times? three? four? the tall piece, the one with the woman standing in a rain of toothpicks—I did that the week we thought you had AIDS....*

"You want to go to San Francisco?" he asked. "Quebec? San Antonio? Tell me—I made a lot of money tonight." He tried to picture them walking a windy hill that overlooked San Francisco Bay, but then he reminded himself that she could hardly walk. Fine, he'd wheel her in a chair. But the wind would make her ill. Then he'd get her a blanket, he'd buy her a goddamn parka, he'd make it happen one way or the other.

"Vancouver appeals to me," she said. "You get both the mountains and the ocean."

As if there weren't time to visit the mountains first and the ocean later. Did she think like that? Since her treatment started, this was something they hadn't talked about: time. Their polite silence about things that mattered told him how truly scared she was, how she must have heard moment by moment the dreadful ticking, how she must have been watching day turn to night, the shadows growing longer.

"Just a minute," he said. He left her abruptly and strode to the file cabinet in the hall closet where her winter coats hung, their mustiness reminding him of snow and days with little light. If he lingered here, it would overwhelm him, the thought of her things remaining in her absence, her absence like a never-ending winter's day, bruised clouds crowding the sky.

Quickly he returned to Sarah's bed with a map of North America. "Let's take a look at Vancouver."

It's what they needed, he thought, some dreams, a picture that might conjure relief, if only for a moment. But Sarah was fading. He knew the look well by now, how fatigue weighed on her so heavily she could hardly speak.

"I've got to go," she said. "I'm sorry. We'll look in the morning, we'll make plans."

She burrowed under her blankets and was suddenly sleeping so deeply he wasn't sure he could have wakened her if he'd had to. Bitterly he thought it too much like a rehearsal for what now seemed the inevitable. She'd been undergoing two-week cycles of treatment, with two-week respites—vacations, she called them—to allow her bone marrow to replenish itself. This week was a vacation. Sleep.

He sat a while and watched her, hearing through the open window the whoop of a car alarm down the block, the passing of traffic, a car horn bleating now and then, a police copter sputtering somewhere in the vicinity. Through all of this he heard, too, her labored breathing.

It was then that he felt panic rise within him and wing haphazardly like a bird trapped in an attic. He looked to the blank-faced TV, then to the wall above Sarah, where she'd hung one of her mother's photos, a picture of an old woman squinting at the sun as if to question the audacity of its heat—Sarah thought it funny.

Snatching a pencil from the nightstand, he began sketching on the back of the map. A new sculpture had come to him: a woman sleeping on a bed of nails. But the nails would be fork tines—hundreds of forks, their crowns jutting from a grassy layer of blue excelsior. And the sleeping woman would be a fluid sculpting of old clothes, silk scarves for her arms, a neat stack of tri-folded handkerchiefs for her feet. Her face would be the blue porcelain plate he'd been saving for a special piece. For this piece. And what else? It needed something more. He regarded Sarah again, his model, his animus, watched her eyelids flutter, her open mouth take in air, a reflex as ancient as the lungfish. He began folding the map he'd been using as sketchpad; the paper, as large as a coverlet, rattled, resisting his efforts. He folded it to book size, the creases all-wrong to make it look overused; then boldly with pencil he circled Vancouver. He'd place this in the sleeping woman's hand, he decided, the map like a note, an announcement of her quiet longing to be elsewhere.

a Handful of Nails

Unbeknownst to the children, I added wood shavings to their turnip stew last night: pine to be exact, which I grated meticulously as if it were a hard cheese. At my most desperate, I've had to do such things because my children, like most children, don't understand deprivation, they understand only their own appetites—which is what makes children so appealing. They are all desire, wide-eyed and voracious.

"Mama, can I have this?" asks Lori, my eleven-year-old.

She holds in both hands for my inspection an oil-soaked sock, which looks, I suppose, delectable. Her siblings are watching her hopefully. Recently they made a meal of wallpaper paste—a glutinous soup, heavily salted and peppered—and only the three youngest got sick. The others sat around afterwards and pretended not to gloat, though they looked very pleased with themselves. I suspect they all suffered stomach cramps.

Lori's my serious one, the child who looks most like me, a small crooked nose, green-green eyes, a swanlike neck but the stocky build of a field hockey player. She knows better than to eat a sock; it's obviously a sock. But the odorous oil, dark as molasses, might have her fooled; I recall how the heady smell of gasoline often tantalized me as a child.

"No," I tell her, "you can't have this."

I take the sock from her, having to tug it from her grasp, then I toss it into the fireplace, where last night's embers ignite the sock in a splendid burst of blue flame. Lori weeps, hands over her eyes as if painfully blinded. The others join her. And I have a roomful of sobbing children. Thirteen, to be exact.

Some nights I dream that I cut off my left arm for the children's dinner and roast it for hours like a succulent leg of lamb, basting it with a thick gravy of my own blood, the house redolent with its sweet baking. I'm not usually inclined to thoughts as melodramatic as that, but the war itself is melodrama and all of us feel the strain. My husband, gone over a year now, was drafted by the bullies of the Revolutionary Militia and my eldest son, Lofe, only fifteen, joined shortly thereafter because, I fear, he liked the look of the uniforms. Families, I've heard, have resorted to eating their house pets, something we don't have, fortunately, and a number of children have run away because, apparently, they felt they'd find better elsewhere.

Had you asked me when I was a teenager, what would become of my life, I would have told you any number of fantasies, none of which have come true. I was good at math and took for granted that I would be a scientist. It would be too easy to say that love did me in, but I must admit that, for a time, love made it seem that being in love was enough. When I met Marcel at the two-year polytech, where those of us without connections or money went, he was by no means the handsomest or the smartest. To speak the truth, I was the smartest in our class of six hundred.

Marcel (pronounced MAR-cel because he thought Mar-CEL too effeminate) is a thoroughly good man, not the type to play hard-to-get nor the type to tell you one thing when he means another. In other words, he was not the type I was attracted to. The uncertainty other young men cultivated, their callous disregard of my feelings, their adolescent self-absorption, made for an edgy excitement that I'd almost found addicting. I had dated about twenty boys before I met Marcel, who sat next to me in calculus. At first I thought his lack of guile was an act, the way he'd blink at me and say, "Don't you look lovely today!" After we started going out, I realized that he was eminently trustworthy. It was such a novelty to be with someone like that; soon I couldn't imagine being with anyone else.

Love sneaked up on me, it seemed, threw a hood over my head, kidnapped me. I found myself doing things I never imagined I'd do, like opening a small computer-repair business with Marcel instead of going on for a degree in advanced mathematics, like living in a city flat instead of a country home where I might have awakened every morning to birdsong instead of bus horns, like having fourteen children instead of two. Sometimes I feel buoyed by my children as, during my girlhood summers, I felt buoyed by our too-salty sea—there is a comfort in my crowd of family. But increasingly I have a fear of the depths my feet cannot reach. Call it a fear of drowning.

What will become of us?

"Metal Man! Metal Man!" the children start screaming. They are clustered at the window. No tears now. The Metal Man, as they call him, is an officer of the Revolutionary Militia who makes the rounds once a week—unannounced—to collect metal for the RM's weaponry. It is the citizenry's job to gather an offering of nails, shrapnel, rebar, tin cans, anything for the cause. And heaven help you if the Officer finds a cooking pot hidden in your kitchen.

"Get your nails," I tell the children. We spend a couple of hours every morning picking through the debris of the latest bombings, of which there are many lately. While the children, under the close supervision of my most responsible—Lori, Nadia and Simon—scavenge for metal scrap, nails from wallboard and aluminum from window frames, I scavenge for copper wire and, if I am especially lucky, terminal boards, relay switches, network junctions, PC monitors. You never know what you'll find.

The metals officer—his family name is Hermes, an alteration of a compromising ethnic name, I suppose— wears an aluminum stewpot, which he's fashioned, through prodigious hammering, into a helmet. It bears a high, scratchy shine and sits a little too low on his head. He is a surprisingly young man, younger than I, to be exact, with one of those sweet rosy faces, whiskers only on his chin. I wonder what is wrong with him that he isn't in the fighting.

The children open the door before he knocks. He bows ever so slightly when he sees me. I think he finds me somewhat attractive, though I don't know why, a mother of fourteen. I've lost weight, it's true, and I've noticed that a streak of gray at my left temple, which seems to have appeared overnight, gives me a haunted look, the kind of startled allure you might expect of the heroine of a romance novel.

Since his visit last week, Officer Hermes has lost another tooth up front. Bad diet, I think. He's always chewing on toffee. His increasing toothlessness gives him a goofy look, like one of those retarded beggars I'd see on the Avenue of the Saints every morning on the way to the market. Before the war. There is no market now, except the black market, friends of friends who know friends who can get you this or that for the right price or barter.

"Good morning, kiddies, what gifts have you for me today?" He holds open his canvas bag like a child at Halloween, his jaw working a wad of toffee.

"Can we have some candy?" the children whine. I think of chicks in a nest, always hungry, mouths gaping. The children grasp at the officer's shiny polyester shirt, his leather belt, his rubber boots, his new blue jeans, which seem proof that he's keeping some collections for himself.

He's well fed, anybody can see, a little paunch above his belt. Something I'd like to punch, just to feel how soft it really is.

"Where would I get candy?" he says cheerfully.

"You're eating it!" they shout in unison.

"You're an official!" Nadia says. "You can get anything!"

That's the problem, I've decided, the "officials" of the world assuming more than their fair share.

"Get your nails," I tell the children again. Each child has a few handfuls and, as usual, we make a production of our offering, the children parading one after the other to the Officer's open bag. As the nails accumulate, their collective noise like the sound of someone going through a change purse, I think of the money Marcel and I hoarded before he was forced to join the RM—big paper bills which featured the President's smiling face over the slogan that made him popular so many years ago: "Let's grow smart, let's grow rich!" I try not to think of the many ways I could have spent our horde before it became worthless. Now the bills paper our leaky wall seams, and my children are wearing sandals I've fashioned from videocassette cases and package string. Boys and girls alike wear shifts I've stapled together from plastic shower curtains. I failed them.

"Nice, very nice," Officer Hermes is saying, nodding his head agreeably at each handful of nails.

Just then we hear a crash from the kitchen and I fear the worst, that Lori has not finished hiding the cookware.

The Officer looks up abruptly, like an alerted guard dog. "Sounded like a pan to me."

"That would be surprising," I say.

He purses his lips at me, suppressing a smile. "Let's take a look."

The children surround him, waving their hands and hopping in protest. "We don't have any pans!" "We're not hiding!" "Nobody's in there!" All of which make a convincing show of our guilt. Still, I can't help but love the children for trying.

When Officer Hermes opens the kitchen door, whose hinges are solid brass, by the way (such are the details that our dull-witted Officials overlook), Lori is at the kitchen sink scrubbing a plastic bowl furiously.

"Little Miss, why aren't you out here to greet me?" Officer Hermes sounds like a storybook character. A wolf or an unctuous ogre.

"I'm being punished," Lori says matter-of-factly, "because I tried to eat a sock this morning."

Officer Hermes nods his head agreeably as if this made sense. That metal-heavy canvas bag at his shoulder, he strolls the length of the kitchen, sizing it up like a prospective tenant; then he opens the stove, which we haven't used in months since there's no gas. Major appliances will be the next thing to go, I suppose.

"I could use these oven racks," he says.

The children crowd around us. They are silent, watchful.

"You think we'll never cook with gas again?" I say. "Is that what you're saying, that the quality of life under the RM—provided the RM wins—will be so meager?"

The Officer rights himself, his face flushed: "I didn't say anything like that. Life will be better, everybody knows life will be better. But first—" he glances at the children as if to warn them, "but first we have to finish winning the war, don't we? We can't hold back, can we? Everybody has to sacrifice, don't they?"

Finish winning the war. How careful he is.

"We sacrifice plenty," says Simon, aware of the implicit blame.

"Bring a written order from Home Base," I say, "and we'll give you our oven racks."

"I don't need a written order," says Officer Hermes. Why is he suddenly angry? Do we threaten him somehow? "I have the mandate to take anything that can be spared."

"You've got plenty from us already," I insist. Now I'm getting angry, though I realize that an argument's only going to put the family at a disadvantage. Calm the man, I tell myself. Flatter him. "You're right, Officer Hermes, you can do anything you please, but today's not the day for oven grills. Tomorrow maybe."

The young man looks at me for a moment as if trying to determine the depth of my disdain. Perhaps my motherly authority daunts him; perhaps he wants me to respond to his male charm, whatever he thinks that may be. In any event, he stoops into the open oven and pulls out the two racks.

"This will suffice," he says.

Why I start crying at this point is complicated. I've never respected women who resort easily to tears, and I myself usually have a tremendous reserve of patience. In this instance, however, I feel overwhelmed—so much has been taken from me already, I can see myself and the children reduced to living in a burned-out bus, as I've heard some families have resorted to doing on the east side of the Capital.

When the fighting started, I was convinced that life under the RM would be no different from life under the PM, and Officer Hermes seems to epitomize my conviction. This candy-mouthed, potbellied, soft-shouldered boy of a man has the gall to stand in my kitchen and, without a twinge of compunction or conscience, take from me, take from my children. And it's just the start, isn't it?

My face covered with my hands, I try to retrieve my tears with a ragged breath—I don't want to give the Officer the satisfaction of my anguish.

"What's this?" I hear him say. "How *dare* you!"

I look: one of the children, Tomin, has smacked him in the back of the neck with a wooden spoon. Before I can admonish Tomin, Nadia strikes him with a small fist in the stomach and then—a horror to behold—the children fall upon the man, pummeling him. He's so surprised, he offers no resistance, only covers his face with his arms and shouts, "Oh!" And I'm so shocked it takes me a moment—no more than a moment, I swear—to yell at the children: "Stop right this minute!" But this hardly sounds strong enough. I start pulling them away. They are furious. Have my tears incited them? "Please stop!" I'm screaming through the rain of fists. The man is down, balled up on the floor. Again I hear him say, "Oh!" The children themselves are hollering a babble of protest: I hear "candy!" "give me!" "unfair!" "nasty!"

I peel the children away, so furious I lash out with one arm, smacking Nadia across the mouth. She wails in pain and this brings the children to attention at last. They fall back, panting, several of them teary-eyed, noses runny. Nadia's lower lip is bloody. Lori dabs at it with the wet cloth she was using at the sink earlier.

I stoop to help up Officer Hermes but he won't budge, balled up as if he feared for his life, though certainly the children's attack, while painful, was hardly life-threatening. I am reminded of those histrionic soccer players who make a show of their injury on the field in order to stop the game and gain everyone's attention. Big babies, I've always thought.

An apology is half out of my mouth—"Officer Hermes, please understand how upset the children are"— when I realize that the man has passed out and yet managed, at the same time, to hold this pose. Is that possible? "Get some water," I say.

One of the children brings over a full glass and, before I can take it from her, dumps it over Officer Hermes's helmeted head.

"A lot of good that does!" I yell. "Get some more."

I unfold the fainted man; the children won't back away, fascinated. I put my ear to his mouth, a finger to his neck, a hand on his chest. Nothing. I do this again. Nothing. I tilt his head back, with two fingers clear his mouth— toss away a half-chewed toffee—depress his tongue, then give him a good breath, mouth-to-mouth, for a few seconds, watch his chest rise: no obstructions, he can breathe just fine but he's *not* breathing. Then I check his pulse. Nothing. The man is dead! I straddle him, my hands on his chest; I pump the heart, one-two-three, one-two-three. Wake up! I scramble back around, his head in my lap, clear his throat, blow life into him again. Then back to his chest, pump and pound. Wake up!

Drastic measures, I'm thinking, this is a time of drastic measures, what will they do to us, set an example? shrug it off as an accident? did he have a prior medical condition?

I'm at his mouth again when he abruptly comes to life, bucking as if from a prod of electricity. One of the children screams. The others back away. Officer Hermes has rolled to his side in a fit of coughing and gasping. I'm weeping again, this time with relief. I stand up, tell the children to give the man some room, then I help Officer Hermes to his feet. He's panting, one hand to his chest, his watery eyes wandering from side to side, his helmet askew.

"What time is it?" he croaks.

"Morning," I tell him.

He looks at me in a dreamy-groggy way, then half smiles. "Is lunch ready?"

"Not yet," I tell him, "come back later." Humor the man.

He shakes his head in wonderment. "I have an appetite for something Italian. Manicotti maybe?"

"Here's some water." Lori offers him a glass.

He takes it, holds the glass to his nose, sniffs once, then hands it back. "Thanks."

"Here's your bag." Simon tries to hand it to him.

"Goodness," he says, "it's heavy, isn't it?"

"Full of nails," says Simon.

"A silly thing to carry around all day, don't you think?" the Officer says cheerfully. The children nod in agreement. They look frightened.

One hand on his hot back, I escort Officer Hermes to the door.

"When did you say lunch was ready?"

"Later, Officer."

Brain damage, I'm thinking. A serious rupture of synapses.

"We should do this again sometime," he says at the open door.

"Next week," I tell him. "You visit us every week, don't you remember?"

I'm wondering who saw him enter, who will see

him leave; can his injury be traced back to us?

"Every week," he echoes. He's staring at the car-sized crater in the center of our street. "Shouldn't we do something about that hole?"

"I'm going to plant flowers in it," I say.

"Nice." He's nodding at thought. "Let me know if I can help. I like dahlias."

As soon as he's on the stoop, I slam the door shut. I'm trembling, a headache crashing through my skull like storm waves. The children are crowded at the window, watching the Officer.

"Get away from there," I bark. "Redding, what are you chewing—what's in your mouth?"

He swallows before I can investigate but, of course, I know toffee when I smell it. A few others are chewing too. Pickpockets!

"You should be ashamed of yourselves," I scold them. "The man almost died."

"He wanted to take our oven," says Redding.

"Our oven grills," Tomin corrects.

"He was going to turn us in," says Lori.

"He wouldn't give us any candy."

"Selfish old man."

"Is he coming back?"

"If he comes back we won't let him."

"He'll report us."

"If he comes back we'll kill him."

"Shut up!" I snap. "Don't *any* of you talk about killing *any*body or *any*thing."

"You kill mice."

"And pigeons."

"And crickets."

Things we've been eating lately when lucky enough to trap them.

"Did you *hear* me?" I say in the manner that silences them. "I didn't raise a household of homicides."

"Nasty man," one of them mutters.

"Get your tools, we're going out," I tell them.

Their tools are sticks, plastic prods, arm-long scraps of lumber for leverage, anything that helps them dig through debris. It's dangerous work and I don't like how common it has become for us, but I have to keep them busy—in their boredom they've nearly torn apart our flat.

I am more than dismayed when, a few minutes later, I discover Officer Hermes sitting on our stoop. He looks up at me, blinks his boyish eyes, half-smiles his goofy smile. He says, "Where're you going?"

"Step around him," I instruct the children, who march out double file.

It's an overcast, blustery day. I hear intermittent mortar fire on the wind, the RM blasting the PM, probably. On the north side. We're on the east where only errant fire finds us. Nothing of importance here.

I say, "We have errands, Officer." He is most definitely a different man.

"Can I go?" he asks.

"Can we stop you?"

He smiles again. "I don't think so; I'm an Official."

"Don't you want your bag?" He's left it on the stoop.

He waves away my concern. "Too heavy."

The children regard the canvas bag longingly, all those nails we could sell to a scrapper. By the time we return, someone will have stolen it, you can be sure.

We walk to the business district a few blocks east, the children chanting the multiplication table in time to their marching.

It looks like everyone's out today with their tools and tote bags, their hand-wagons and shopping carts. I've seen some people collect any- and everything they can find, no matter how worthless: fractured bricks, grapefruit-sized chunks of asphalt, handfuls of shattered glass. Something's better than nothing, they must think.

The scavenging has gotten so bad, none of our buildings has doorknobs or door handles or stoop banisters anymore, metal is so valuable; it's made for suspicious neighbors. Who would steal the knob off your front door?

"Look at this," Officer Hermes says. He's yanking at the door of a gutted Minotaur automobile. "It's a gold mine!"

The children laugh at him. Everyone knows—or almost everyone—that the metal of the Minotaur is so poor in quality it's not worth recycling. You'd do better to strip the plastic, which somebody has already done.

"Help me out here," the Officer exclaims.

I don't want to see the man have another heart attack, so I order the children to unhinge the car door, which they do easily, their many little hands adept at close work.

"The door's enough," I tell the Officer. He's hefted the thing onto his back.

"It's heavier than it looks," he says. Or he's weaker than he knows.

Though it's a cool day, he's sweating, too flushed from exertion. "Stay away from his pockets," I tell the children. I see their mouths working on toffee. Who knows what else they have lifted? The man's belt is missing. "Who's got his belt?" I demand, but the children ignore me and march on, chanting, "*Eleven times eleven makes one hundred twenty-one, twelve times twelve makes...*"

"You could leave the door here," I tell the Officer, "and we'll pick it up on the way back."

"Do you think I'm that simple?" Hunched over like an old man, he peers up at me from under his burden. He is trudging behind us with an uncertain step.

"To tell the truth, Officer, that door is worthless."

"It feels like more than that," he says.

"The manufacturer weights them with composite sludge—that's what makes them so heavy."

"It feels *very* heavy."

"But it's worthless."

"Nothing that weighs this much could be worthless."

The man's going to kill himself, I'm thinking.

"Let's dig here," I announce. It's not an especially promising site, a few low-rises that have been reduced to heaps of wallboard and mortar, but I want to give the Officer a rest.

The children look at me in question.

"Here," I repeat. "Group Alpha take the northeast quadrant. Betas take the southeast and so on." We always work clockwise and alphabetically. My attempt at giving them some structure.

"I'll guard the door," Officer Hermes says.

"That's not necessary," I say.

He sets the door down gingerly, then lies across it as if it were a cot, resting on his side, his hands as a pillow.

"Are you all right?" I ask.

"Just a little nap," he says.

"Maybe you should go home."

"I can't move another inch."

I lean forward, close to his flushed face. He won't open his eyes. "Do you have a condition?" I grab at what I think is a medical alert bracelet on his left wrist, but it turns out to be only an ID bracelet, solid silver. It says, "Hermes."

Again I ask him, this time more loudly: "Do you have a condition?"

"Very tired," he mutters. "A few minutes."

"Don't die!"

He opens his eyes. "Am I dying?"

"It *looks* that way," I say quietly.

"I don't *feel* like I'm dying."

"I think it's a heart attack, Officer."

"That won't do," he says. He tries to sit up but can't find the strength. He gasps. "That won't do at all. I can't die." Panicked, he gazes up at me like a spooked child.

Instinctively I lay an open hand on his forehead. "Just relax. We'll get you help."

The children have crowded around again.

"If he's dying," says Lori, "we should leave him here."

"But take his boots," says Tomin, "they look like new."

How have my children grown so callous under my care?

"Enough, children!" I instruct them to lift the car door, which we'll use as a stretcher. They whine about the burden.

"He's too fat," one of them says.

"I've tried to diet," Hermes replies feebly. "And I'm walking all day."

"Sometimes it's simply a matter of heredity," I tell him. "Simon, keep your end up." Simon sighs.

By the time we get Officer Hermes to a Security kiosk, many blocks from our flat, it's dark. Although he's still conscious, Hermes looks like a corpse, lying on his back, hands folded on his chest, his eyes open to the sky. The several times we've stopped to rest I have checked his pulse and found it wildly erratic. "Don't speak," I've instructed. "Think of snow. White, quiet, blankets of snow."

"I'm thinking of popcorn," he said, "acres and acres of popcorn."

At last, the children groaning with fatigue, we have set him and the car door in an arc of yellow light just outside the kiosk. This is our ultimate scavenge, I think ruefully.

"Where are his pants?" the Security Officer wants to know. He's a florid old man with a handlebar mustache. He wears a dirty baker's uniform and, on his narrow head, a cracked white bicycle helmet.

He's so distracted he doesn't seem to mind my children crowding around him, their hands reaching for his whistle, the stripes sewn onto his filthy tunic, the sommelier's cup dangling from his neck.

Besides his blue jeans, Officer Hermes is missing several other personal items: his boots, his shiny pot-helmet, his belt, his socks.

"This man's half naked!" the Security Officer says.

"I don't know what to tell you," I say. "You can't put anything down these days without somebody picking over it."

"You put him down?"

"Many times," I say with regret. "He's heavier than he looks."

"I will have to write a report," he says.

I sigh. "Of course you will."

The Security Officer regards his fallen comrade sadly. "He was one of our best collectors, you know."

"Oh, yes, he's good at his job," I say. "Children, leave the Security Officer alone." They have pulled his stripes off of one arm.

"He died in the line of duty, I'll put that in my report."

"He's not dead!" I say. God forbid that he die in our care.

"What's that?"

"No, I'm not dead," says Officer Hermes.

The Security Officer flinches: "Good God! What are you doing, man?"

Officer Hermes smiles up at him politely. "I had a heart attack, I think."

The Security Officer smooths down his mustache, takes a deep breath, reassumes his calm: "How did that happen?"

"Years of bad diet, I'm afraid, and not enough exercise—"

"Or it could be a matter of heredity," I remind him.

"No, I mean what brought it on."

"He overexerted himself," I say. "In the line of duty, I should add. He was trying to carry a car door."

"Car doors aren't worth anything."

"Apparently Officer Hermes doesn't know that."

"Ridiculous," the old man huffs. He glares down at Hermes. "Don't you know enough not to take a car door?"

"Apparently not," Hermes sighs. "Will this go on my record?"

"I should say so." The Security Officer sounds disappointed. "I'll have to write a report." He starts opening drawers, searching for paper, I suppose. His computer terminal looks dead. Not enough AC apparently.

The children are entreating him: "You got candy in here?" "Can I see that cup?" "Where'd you get that whistle?"

Officer Hermes says to me, "I feel so stupid."

"You were just trying to do your job." I surprise myself that I can be so kind to this man who was so recently unkind to me. Sermonizers on the radio encourage the belief that the war brings out the best in each of us, but this is only wishful thinking. Most of what I've seen has been less than ideal. Neighbors avoid one another—we have never been more distant—because everyone's panicked by the shortages. No one wants to be put in the position of having to surrender what little he or she has hidden, hoarded, salvaged or stolen.

"May we go now?" I say at last.

The old man looks up, half-startled, as if I've just awakened him from a nap. "I'll need your signature."

"On what?" I can't remember the last time I wrote my signature. Paper is impossible to come by, except for the few books of Marcel's I've been saving. And worthless money.

"Here, write it on my sleeve." He produces a ballpoint pen, one of those cheap plastic kind that always leak when they're half empty.

I sign a pseudonym—Madame Bovary—hardly legible on his tunic sleeve, he nods in satisfaction, trying to read my scrawl; then I leave abruptly, my children flooding around me. I'm so weary, so confused by the events of the day.

"Children, tell Officer Hermes good-bye."

"Can you make that farewell?" asks Hermes.

I instruct the children to do so. Reluctantly they oblige. Minutes later, as we're walking away, Lori says, "He's going to die, I bet anything."

"Yeah, he's meat," says Tomin.

"I won't miss him."

"Have some compassion," I scold them. "He's a sick man."

"If he wasn't sick, would you have compassion, Mama?"

"That's too hard a question to answer right now," I admit.

My honesty quiets them for a while, like a drop cloth over a cage of finches.

Ahead of us is the canyon of the darkened avenue, the dull orange flicker of candle flame in a few windows of the apartment buildings that loom on either side; I smell wood smoke. Surprising that I hear no distant gunfire. From somewhere nearby, but not on this street, someone's playing a recording of Cole Porter's "Begin the Beguine," a dreamy romantic tune.

"We didn't get any scrap today," Simon complains.

"I guess we'll have to work extra hard tomorrow," I say.

The children groan in chorus. It's a pleasure hearing their collective voice: it buoys me a bit.

"Watch your step," I remind them. "Who's in the lead?"

Suddenly, from the gloom ahead, I hear a shrill note, loud and piercing like an alarm. One of my children has stolen the Security Officer's whistle.

Still Life

A high-ceilinged room that reeks of turpentine, the art studio is drafty, especially now in late October, and sometimes Dom has to concentrate to keep from shivering. Every twenty minutes a student repositions the heater for him. Still, by the end of the three-hour session, his feet and hands will be pale blue from the chill, his buttocks clammy, his genitals withdrawn almost wholly into himself. But he likes the work, as difficult as it is, because when he sits naked before the students, he feels comforted, as if their scrutiny were a kind of care.

Sadowski, the teacher, paces at the back of the room, as always, a foot-long paintbrush in hand. She wears jeans and black high-tops and a paint-splattered smock that she's had since she was a student herself twenty years ago. She says, "Paint with your eyes, people, not with your head."

Dom notices a student staring at his right foot so intently, the boy seems to long for it. No one, not even Amanda, has gazed at him so closely, so seriously. It's flattering, really. He feels remarkable. Priceless.

If his friends, his colleagues, his acquaintances, knew what he was doing, they would be appalled, convinced that he is overcompensating for his loss. See a counselor, they would advise. His own doctor, a man who has known him for eleven years, told him that he would probably experience severe depression, even consider suicide, before he regained his equilibrium and "viewed the horizon again as an unwavering line."

Randal, his brother, phones once a week. Ever since their parents died eleven years ago—his mother of a heart attack, his father of a stroke—Randal has been chummy, completely forgetting the rivalry of their early years. He owns a successful chain of miniature golf courses in southern California and can talk of little besides golf, Amanda's game: "She said I had a good long shot, remember?"

"You don't have to do this," Dom told him.

"I'm a good sport, she said. Probably because I never threw a club. Unlike you, big brother." Randal's attempt at teasing.

When Dom let the conversation die finally, Randal said, "It helps to talk about it, you know."

Amanda's friends, most retired now to the Southwest, still phone, five months after the funeral: "Anything you need, Dom...." His own friends phone too, some from faraway places: "Come to our time-share in Maui, Dom. Stay as long as you like. Lie on the beach like a rock. ..."

Their overweening concern suggests that he will decline rapidly. He needs watching. So they have crowded his house with fruit baskets, his mailbox with kindly-worded cards and notes, invitations to dinners that promise to be like wakes themselves, everyone pretending heroically that nothing is wrong. But, of course, everything is wrong—he's a sixty-seven-year-old, childless widower. What's left for him but quiet days of long walks, of reading and gardening, of occasional games of bridge with people who have known him too long and cannot conceive of him doing anything other than this: playing a conservative and disinterested hand, eating chocolate-covered peanuts, and letting his mind wander while waiting for the next bid?

If Dom chose to explain himself now, what would he say?

His bottom burns, as if chafed. This always happens after the first hour of sitting. Soon it will be numb. Then his lower back will ache. After that, his hamstrings will tighten, then his calves, his neck, his shoulders. During these past two months of studio work, he has mapped out the many aches and pains. Always they arrive in the same sequence, at about the same intervals, and somehow this predictability is comforting.

Today, however, something new has announced itself: his right elbow is tingling, going numb. If it were his left, he'd have cause to worry, wouldn't he, because it was the left that Steve Farmer complained about just before he keeled over from heart failure on the golf course last year: "Must've pulled it when I was practicing my drive," Farmer said, shaking his head in disbelief, as if it were a joke. "Guess I'm getting old." He was sixty-four. Died before the ambulance arrived. Grass on the fairway still hasn't grown back completely where the tires spun as the truck sped off, lights flashing, siren whooping.

But Dom's pain is in the right arm. And he hasn't been leaning on it. He recalls his activities today; has he bumped something?

"Mr. Kezur, you're fidgeting." This from Erin, a young woman with a pale, freckled face and a boyish haircut. Her painting has made him look like a storm-ravaged King Lear. "Is that really me?" he asked her earlier. She shrugged in response, dabbing her brush at her palette. She said, "A better question is, does it matter, Mr. Kezur?"

He has asked the students to call him by his first name, but none of them has, even though he's made a point of learning theirs. There are seventeen students in the class, all of them art majors, most of them seniors. Whenever he passes them on campus, he calls out to them and usually they return his greeting, though it seems they aren't sure who he is. The campus is big, twenty-five thousand students, so he can understand their confusion. Maybe they don't recognize him with his clothes on.

Next to Erin stands Lionel, a portly kid with a spotty beard and a frizzy ponytail. It seems he has taken pleasure in making Dom ugly, emphasizing in his portrait the turkey wattle of Dom's throat, the bruise-blue bags under his eyes, the wrinkles of his face like sun-ruined mud. To the boy he appears no more than a grotesque curiosity, a study in the awful effects of aging. Recently, Dom said to him, with pronounced sarcasm: "You've really captured me heart and soul, Lionel." The boy nodded yes, yes, thank you, pausing to appraise his work. Then, as if to compliment Dom, he said, "I've never had a subject like you, Mr. Kezur." And Dom knew he meant to say, I've never painted anyone so old.

Then there is Stone, a tall whiskerless kid with a crew cut. He paints with vividly unreal colors and has, to Dom's regret, made him look like a ghost, a transparent wash of yellowed flesh. *Look at me!* Dom wants to shout. *Two-hundred-forty pounds—do I appear so insubstantial?*

These are the only three students he can see directly, positioned as he is, without his glasses. He sits on small riser at the center of the room, a towel draped over the too-narrow stool that he has never bothered to replace, even though he promised himself a more comfortable seat after the pain of his first sitting. Privately, he's proud that he's gotten used to it. This isn't for everyone.

But he has spent his life sitting, hasn't he? Sitting at a desk in his windowed office, at Trotter, Manning, and Kezur Insurance, for twenty-seven years; sitting in his recliner in the den at home, with the TV on; sitting in the golf cart while he watched Amanda play her expert's game; then sitting at her bedside in the hospital, where she shared a room with a stroke victim who kept saying to no one in particular, "Help me, honey, help me, honey," like the refrain of a sad song.

As Dom held Amanda's cool hand, he wondered if she remembered their talk about death, how they had vowed to help each other elude the painful wait. They had anticipated that the bad things—paralysis, say, or dementia—wouldn't happen until their late seventies or sometime in their eighties.

"My greatest fear," Dom had confessed, "is that I won't know I'm going bad until it's too late, until I've lost my ability to tell how bad I really am. By then, I'll be a drooling idiot whose bottom you'll have to wipe."

"I'll take care of you," Amanda promised. "Don't worry." This was last spring. Or the spring before last. Dom isn't sure. Nor can he remember how they had started the conversation, but Amanda welcomed the subject without hesitation. He recalls thinking that this was how she ran her life, addressing each obstacle or problem as she addressed the ball at the tee: there it lies, here you stand, keep your head down, follow through with your swing...

They were sitting in white wicker chairs on the patio. Amanda was squinting up at him, the morning glare in her well-sunned face, which had not changed much over the years: full cheeks, her eyes a little too wide apart, her blunt nose always red and peeling from too much sun.

Dom said, "I don't want you to *take care* of me, Amanda, I want you to put me to *sleep.*" Why couldn't he say it more bluntly?

"That's what I mean," she said. "I'll feed you some pills. Then I'll take some myself."

He pictured her standing over his bed, where he'd be sleeping his way to death, the half-empty bottle of pills in her hand. How horrible to be the conscious one, alone at last, too aware of the empty house, the hum of the refrigerator, the shudder of the furnace as it blows heat through the rattling vents, the tick of the floorboards as they expand—she'd think of the mail waiting in the box outside, of the lights on in other rooms, of the water dripping from the kitchen faucet, everything waiting for her hand, everything beckoning her back to life. How could she find the strength to join him?

He said, "I wouldn't want you to *join* me like that, Amanda. Maybe you'll be healthy, maybe you'll have plenty of good living left." He put a hand on her shoulder, as if to steady her, though he was the one who felt lightheaded.

She smiled her only smile, which some people mistook for a smirk. She said, "I don't think so, Dom."

They had just moved into a customized split-level adjacent to the eighth green of the Ravenhill Golf Course.

Their retirement home. Amanda promised to teach him, once and for all, how to be a good golfer or at least good enough to keep up with her. They soon discovered that although their neighborhood was "well-appointed," their house had not been well placed: mornings, afternoons, and evenings, wayward golf balls clattered onto their roof, bounded from their flagstone patio, and dropped abruptly into their backyard.

It was after being struck by one such ball, while she was weeding the flowers out back, that Amanda had gone to the hospital for x-rays. And it was then that the doctors discovered a tumor in her brain.

They could only "core" the tumor, which would give her more time, said the doctors, "though we can't say how much more. Maybe a year, maybe five, it's hard to predict."

After the operation, it was surprising how quickly she declined. She spent her last days golfing at Ravenhill. It depressed her because she didn't have strength enough to play well. "I guess this is my worst fear realized," she said after her last nine holes. "I'm too conscious of my own de-cline." She dropped the crumpled scorecard into his lap. He was sitting in the golf cart, mute with grief. She looked defeated, feeble. She was only fifty-eight.

"What are you afraid of?" Sadowski is saying. Dom glances to his right: she's swiping her brush at a student's canvas. "Let go a little, Heather. Give his belly *authority*—swirl some." Sadowski shows her how to stroke her swirls.

The first month of modeling, Dom hoped that Sadowski would invite him home for dinner. Her husband is a theology professor. Dom imagines that they spend their evenings drinking wine and discussing things that matter. But, to Sadowski, Dom is only an employee. She doesn't know anything about him because she hasn't asked any-thing, except why he wants to model. "I'm retired," he told her, after answering the ad he saw posted on the bulletin board at the university hospital the last week of his wife's stay there. "I like art. I believe in education. And, frankly, I want to contribute something to the kids' experience."

Sadowski nodded her head, her silver bangs in her eyes. She said, "You're what I've been looking for, Mr. Kezur."

"Call me Dom, please."

Like the students, she never has.

"Mr. Kezur, your head, please." It's Erin again. She's squinting at him in a way that reminds him of Amanda, how she looked when he asked, in a broken voice, "Do you want me to get you some pills? For sleep?" She had been confined to a bed in the hospital finally, where doctors were attempting last-minute radiation treatment. When Amanda looked at him like that, her eyes narrowed, he wasn't sure what she was thinking. But he knew he wasn't capable, that he wouldn't follow through, no matter how much pain she was suffering.

He nods to Erin to acknowledge her complaint. But she's looking elsewhere, perhaps at his stomach. What do any of them see really? He draws a deep breath and settles again. He is facing left, to the windows, which look out to the quad and the too-sunny afternoon. The weather has been jumpy all fall, alternating from one extreme to the other. They've had snow as early as the first week of October and as recently as two days ago, but all of that has melted and now the sun has elbowed the clouds from the sky and the day has grown almost balmy, some of the kids wearing shorts to class. The greenhouse effect, the students are saying.

Pain snakes through Dom's right arm. It feels like the hot probe of shock racing from his shoulder to the tip of his middle finger. He's panicked a little, his heart speeding. He tries to imagine the source, some short circuit in the web of his nerves. It has to be something minor, some small glitch in the relay of signals inside him.

Sadowski taps her paintbrush handle against somebody's easel rapidly, like a conductor signaling her orchestra: time for a break. The students begin drifting into the hallway and outside to smoke their filterless cigarettes and drink tepid coffee, bought from the vending machine at the other end of the hall where a high window is pearly with afternoon light.

Although he is thoroughly chilled, Dom doesn't immediately throw on his robe, the lovely polished cotton paisley Amanda bought him last year. He is careful of his muscles, his heart especially: he stands only halfway at first, kneading his taut hamstrings and calves with his icy fingertips. Breathing slowly. Calm, he's thinking, stay calm. Then he rises gradually to his full height, reaching for the ceiling, one hand following the other. He yawns—Okay, he's telling himself, you're okay—he blows on his cupped hands, and surveys the room. A few students are still dabbing at their canvases.

The first time he disrobed for the class, he felt exhilarated. It was a triumph of sorts, standing naked like that, and he'd been tempted to raise his clenched fists in defiance, as if to shout, "Here I am, whole, healthy, steamy with life!" It felt dangerous, his exposure. And he was so thrilled suddenly, so taken with this new attention, this new life, he thought he might get an erection.

It was the same feeling he'd had when, years ago, he sat with Lynda Maxwell, one of his wife's competitors, on the couch of a hotel suite, and she lolled in his arms as he kissed her face hungrily. His ears burned, he heard the distant ringing of alarm, and each time he opened his eyes the room nodded as if he were riding ocean swells, sweeping from crest to crest.

Even though he didn't continue the affair—couldn't continue for all his self-loathing—his longing pursued him. He relived his infidelity in memory, every moment slowed so that he could examine it with excruciating appreciation: the way his mouth met Lynda's while his mind screamed, "Don't!", the way his hand smoothed the hair away from her cheek, her hot breath in his ear, even as he pictured Amanda on the fairway, the beauty of her swing as she followed through with a three iron. ... For fourteen years the memories visited him, as seductive and reckless as the initial indiscretion. And all the while he worried that he would call out Lynda's name while talking to Amanda or, worse, while loving her.

A few years ago he heard, from Amanda herself, that Lynda had died of breast cancer. This put a stop to the fantasies finally. And something inside of him—hope?—withered.

"It wasn't painful, was it?" he asked Amanda.

"I don't know how it could have been anything but painful," she said. "It's the number one killer of women, you know."

"How old was she?"

"Fifty-two," said Amanda.

Wearing his robe, his house slippers, his wire-rim eyeglasses, Dom tours the studio, pausing every few steps to stretch a little more. You're okay, he's telling himself, everything is fine. His right arm feels heavier than his left, the senses duller, but it doesn't pain him.

Since Amanda's death, he has worried that he will be next, that one morning a golf ball will rocket through his window like a hand grenade and so startle him that he'll collapse from heart failure. He has put his house up for sale. But the market is slow, his realtor cautions. It will take a year, maybe two, to get a reasonable offer. In the meantime, he stays away from the place as much as possible—it's too full of his past, Amanda's clubs in the garage, her trophies lining the shelves of the living room, her perfume a too-palpable presence every time he passes her closet.

Dom is staring at Heather's painting—she has made him look as pink as a cartoon pig and she has got his stomach all wrong, though Sadowski's swirls, in yellow, have helped fill it out. When Sadowski comes up behind him, Dom is shaking his head in dismay. The room is empty but for the two of them. Dom's face, a partial profile staring back at them from so many canvases, looks like some kind of practical joke, he thinks.

Sadowski says: "This is *Interpretive* Portraiture, don't forget."

"Why don't they see me?" he asks.

She is staring critically at the painting, her arms folded over her chest, the paintbrush in one hand. She says, "You've got to let the students find their own center of gravity, Mr. Kezur."

He wishes she would call him by his first name. Just once.

He says, "You're right, Leslie. Maybe I'm too demanding."

"Who knows," she says, "maybe one of these will end up in the New York Museum of Modern Art someday."

Is this what she dreams of?

Dom looks at her, as if she were a painting herself. For a moment, she is lost in thought, gazing at her student's mediocre work. Then she glances at Dom. His scrutiny has embarrassed her. She smiles. Shrugs, "Oh, well..." Then moves on.

As he steps into the hall to join the students, Dom senses them shift uneasily, too aware of his presence. They don't know what to make of him. Perhaps they think that, having seen him naked, they have compromised him somehow. Perhaps he simply scares them.

Clustered in groups of three or four, the kids talk of movies he's never seen and music he's never heard. They remind him of the beatniks of his day: somberly hip youngsters wearing faded jeans, baggy sweaters or sweatshirts, and scuffed work boots. They are too carefully disheveled, too persistently ironic.

After getting his coffee, he approaches Erin, Lionel, and Stone, who nod a greeting. "Hey, Mr. Kezur," says Erin.

"Call me Dom, please." He offers them a smile. He holds the Styrofoam cup of steamy coffee in his left hand. His right dangles limply at his side. Just resting, he thinks. The wide hallway, which is too dark for his liking, feels colder than the studio. He should wear socks with his sandals. And a heavier robe.

"How come we never see you on campus?" says Stone, an unlit cigarette in his mouth. He offers one to Dom. Dom declines.

"Hey, is this the smoking area?" Lionel asks, trying to make a joke but sounding peevish. Dom knows the type, the boy who tries too hard, the boy nobody really likes.

"Fuck it." Stone lights up, squinting through the smoke.

Dom says, "I'm always on campus. And I've seen *you.*"

"Me?"

"All of you, at one time or another, usually from a distance."

"Did *we* see you? That's the question," says Erin. She stirs her coffee with the sharpened end of a pencil. She's carefully careless in her appearance, Dom notices, her hair teased to look wind-tossed, her shirt untucked but well pressed.

"Well, I waved," he says.

"Did we wave back? That's the other question." Stone blows an oblong smoke ring towards Lionel, who grimaces.

"Sometimes," says Dom. "But maybe you don't recognize me."

"It's a different frame, that's the thing," says Erin. She glances down at her coffee. She doesn't look eager to drink it.

"You mean a different context," says Lionel.

"I mean I don't expect to see him outside class," she says. "In fact, I've *never* seen him outside class."

"I'm on campus every day," Dom insists. He tries to remember if he was like this, so thoughtless, so rude, when he was a youngster.

Erin takes a cigarette from the pack in Stone's sweatshirt pocket. She says, "Thanks for offering, *Stone.*"

He rolls his eyes.

Lionel watches her light up. Dom sees immediately that the boy is in love with her. In fact, he looks sick with longing, his face too pale, his dark-whiskered cheeks gleaming with sweat. Perhaps he plots revenge against the underfed, sardonic Stone, who is clearly Erin's favorite.

Dom sips his coffee. Already it is cool. The group has fallen silent. Dom has this effect on the students; he oppresses them somehow. The voices of others resound above them in the cavernous hallway.

Finally, he says, "Do you like Sadowski's class?" It makes him cringe to hear himself ask such an insipid question.

Lionel shrugs, wiping a paint-speckled hand across his beard. "It's one more road to hoe."

"Row," says Erin. "One more *row* to hoe."

"Whatever."

"I want Sadowski's smock," says Stone. "It's trashed."

"I'd frame the thing if I had it," says Erin. She turns to Lionel. "Or maybe you'd like to context the thing."

"I don't care for her smock," he says. The cigarette smoke makes his eyes water. He sniffs, as if he had a cold. "I'd burn it," he adds.

They fall silent again. There is never enough to say. Dom knows they don't take him seriously. How can they know that he has shelves of art books at home, that he has visited some of the world's greatest art museums, that he cried when he saw the Sistine Chapel? He wants to tell them this, tell all of them what he knows, where he's been, what he's seen.

He says, "Sadowski tells me someday one of your canvases may be hanging in the Museum of Modern Art."

"Did she say which canvas in particular?" Stone asks. He drops the butt of his cigarette into his half-finished coffee. Then he lights another.

"I don't doubt that a lot of our canvases will be hanging in a museum," says Erin. Her cigarette has gone out, still scissored between two fingers. "Problem is, they'll be painted over with someone else's work."

Lionel barks a laugh, which turns into a fit of coughing.

"It wasn't that funny," says Stone. He slaps Lionel on the back. Lionel regains his composure finally, his eyes red from the strain. He seems to have trouble breathing.

Down the hall, students are beginning to gather at the studio door. "About that time," says Dom. He tries to point with his right hand but he can't lift his arm. It's numb.

He feels the blood rush to his face, the light around him growing dimmer, his breath caught short. He's not right. His heart is climbing out of him. He wavers. Do they see what is happening? It—the attack, the failure, the collapse— is now upon him, as sudden as Lionel's coughing fit. Dom wants to cry out for help, but no words come, his tongue like a warm slab of liver in his mouth. He blinks to clear his eyes. Already the kids are ahead of him, crowding at the door. They will go inside, pick up their brushes, begin dabbing at their canvases while he dies out here in the hallway. As simple as that.

In anger, he pursues them and is surprised to discover that his legs work fine. Although he feels dizzy, he suspects that it may be mostly fear. He imagines himself a pilot checking the instrument panel of his damaged craft as he attempts a landing. Coming in on one wing.

He waits for someone to say, "What is it, Dom, are you feeling all right?" He has never walked more slowly, more cautiously, as he approaches the riser.

But his heart settles finally, his face feels cooler, though his right arm is still useless. He turns the word over in his mind—useless. He is sitting now, measuring his breath, registering the changes in his body, taking inventory: he appreciates the flat solidity of his blue-white feet, the baseball-sized knot of each calf muscle, the firm spill of his wide pale belly, the nestlike swirl of gray-black hair between his drooping breasts. He has never been more aware of himself.

"It's snowing," someone announces.

"No way."

"Cool."

"You mean *cold.*"

The students talk as they paint, calling across the room.

Through the tall windows to his left, Dom sees that the sky is crowded with billowy white clouds, which glow silver where the sun is trying to break through.

"I need a ride."

"I need snow tires."

"Chains."

"Don't get kinky."

A few students laugh.

Dom envies their tribal awareness, their easy informality. He disdains his own tribe, the oldsters, their well-established rituals, their sense of decorum, their lives run like a golf tournament, everybody dressed just so, everyone allowed only so many strokes.

"What the hell is *that?*" someone says.

A sudden clatter of hail rains like gravel against the glass of the skylights. "Will it break?" a student asks. No one answers. Sadowski stares skeptically at the ceiling, the students paused with paintbrushes in hand, their young faces upturned anxiously, the drafty room quiet but for the clatter of ice overhead. The noise makes Dom wince, reminding him of home: golf balls hitting his roof.

Then he hears a heavy thump. Startled, it takes him a moment to realize that one of the students has collapsed. It is Lionel, sprawled on his stomach between his own easel and Erin's.

Dom stands up, ready to help. He recalls the boy's pale, worried face, how ill he looked.

"Stand back," Sadowski is saying. She waves the students aside with her brush. Stone helps her turn Lionel over, Lionel's shirt riding over his pale belly, his beltless jeans too low on his hips. They straighten him out, lay the boy's head in Sadowski's lap. She gently pats his jowly face. "Is he diabetic?"

Dom sees Erin shrug. "I don't think so."

"He wasn't looking too good earlier," says Stone.

Sadowski nods. "Probably the flu."

Lionel's eyelids are fluttering, as if he were struggling to resurface. Dom notices that the boy's hands are so dirty with paint they look bruised.

Sadowski asks for two volunteers—Erin and Stone—to help carry Lionel into her office at the back of the studio. As they heft him, the students clearing their easels out of the way, Lionel begins to moan.

"What's he saying?"

"Sounds like 'air raid.'"

Erin, that's what it is, Dom is sure. An admission of love.

Will the boy ever have the nerve to act on his longing? Probably not. He'll wait and worry and watch and, finally, he'll let her drift away. Then he'll waste his time, years maybe, thinking about how alive he felt whenever he dared to stand close to her.

Dom clenches his right hand. Still numb. But maybe it's only the flu. He does feel achy, doesn't he?

Later, at home, Dom opens the windows to air out the sweet stink of rotting fruit, his dining room table crowded with cellophaned gifts of sympathy, which continue to arrive week after week. He throws all of these, baskets included, into two king-sized trash bags, then drags them to the curb for pickup the next day. Outside, it's so sunny, the sky now nearly cloudless, it makes him squint. One would never guess that there were snow flurries and hail earlier. The air smells of wet tree bark and fresh mud, as if spring were imminent and, in fact, the crocuses Amanda planted last summer are beginning to show their white tops in the flower beds on either side of the flagstone walk.

This is just like her. She always left something behind as a reminder while she traveled: a note tacked to the steaks in the freezer, a new bottle of cologne tucked into his sock drawer, a single fresh flower, its petals not yet wilted, taped to the mirror of the medicine cabinet.

Her homecomings are among his favorite memories: how he'd grow anxious as he watched for her in the crowd deplaning, how he'd feel a subtle sting of relief when his eyes found hers finally, how, as they embraced, he'd inhale the stale airplane odor of her clothes, taste the bitter flavor of coffee on her lips, feel her strong fingers pressing at his back.

She was gone nearly every other month, to one tour

nament or another. Some of his friends felt she was gone too much, that a marriage couldn't sustain this kind of absence. But it was the absences that made the marriage work, because each time she and Dom came together again, they had to be gentle with one another. In many ways, it was like starting over. Dom would wake the next morning surprised to find her beside him, almost the way he'd felt after their first night together, sunlight in his eyes, a strand of her auburn hair like a bracelet around his wrist, the perfume of her body warmth, as strong as honeysuckle, drifting to him as he lifted the blankets.

He never confessed his one affair and, if she had heard about it, she never let on. Sometimes—even now—the guilt weighs upon him like a migraine, his head too full of it.

Once, she left him the gift of a new set of golf clubs. Very expensive. "While I'm on tour," she wrote, "you can practice your game. Be kind to yourself!" She knew he didn't have patience for the game and he knew she loved him for trying to play. He practiced dutifully with the new clubs. But one afternoon, after he flubbed a chip shot four times on a par-four hole, he grew so incensed at his inability he dumped the clubs, bag and all, into the nearby water hazard. Later, he retrieved them, though he never found two of his irons. Amanda must have noticed, but she never said a word.

Not long ago she told him this: "When I'm gone, you'll have no trouble finding companionship. Men never do. So I won't worry about you."

"No," he said, "don't worry about me."

He should have clutched her hand, he should have begged her to stay. Begged her. Now the many things he could have said, the many things he wanted to tell her, remain spoken only in memory, like a voice reverberating forever in a cave.

In the distance he hears someone holler: "Fore!"

He flinches, crouching abruptly on a wet flagstone, shielding his head with his hands. He waits for it: the whistle of the rocketed ball. He hears a motorcycle accelerating in the distance. Or maybe it's the whine of a single-engine plane. Then there is silence, except for a breeze rattling the shrubs. Stiffly, he straightens himself finally. He feels foolish. And angry. But no one has seen him; the wide streets are empty.

It isn't until he has gone inside that he realizes his right arm is feeling much better. It functions almost as well as usual. It doesn't ache at all. Clenching and unclenching his right hand, he brings it to his throat, touches his Adam's apple, then swallows. His throat is sore. He isn't sure if this is the ache of relief, of an abruptly choked sob, or simply the onset of the flu. Surely, the weather is to blame. The crazy weather.

From the lace-curtained window over the empty kitchen sinks, he looks out at the backyard and wonders where the golfers are. They'd be out even if it were twenty degrees cooler. The course looks like rolling pasture, still green in patches and yellow-brown elsewhere, with leafless oaks on either side. It bothers him that he can't see the golfers.

He opens the curtains in his den, where he has been sleeping for the past several months, on the couch in front of the console TV. He has never bothered to pull out the sleeper; it's too much work and the couch is plenty wide, his blankets and pillows heaped at one end. The TV is on, murmuring, as always. But he senses that something isn't right. He grows anxious. He feels his heart shudder.

Then he sees it, the sliding glass doors he has just uncurtained. One pane is webbed with cracks, from top to bottom, like ice crazed and splintered by some great weight. And outside, poised on a slate tile—an egg-sized appetizer on a large gray plate—is a golf ball, bright with sunshine.

Dom eases open the door. The glass holds. Not one splinter drops. He recalls how anxious the students were earlier under the rain of hail. Will it break? one of them asked of the skylight.

He hears someone—a woman—humming. It is the

golfer no doubt, as yet unseen, strolling up the slope of his lawn to ask after the wayward shot. When she arrives, she will be taken by the sight, he is sure: "Isn't that something?" she'll say. "I'm sorry about the damage, but you've got to admit that's really something, the way it held, in a thousand tiny pieces." Dom will nod in agreement. "Sure," he'll say, hardly surprised, as if he's understood all his life the physics of things so easily broken.

Garbage

C aptain says we can't dump here because the tide's too strong and will wash everything ashore, which'll catch us hell when we return. So we head out, losing sight of the city, its towers sticking tops through the haze like gray fingertips through dirty rags, like someone drowning in garbage. No one's drowned yet on our run, dangerous as it is, though my mate, Douglas, fell in once when we were dumping and the load dragged him fifty feet down, he said. But he was buoyed up finally by a loose trash bag that had filled with gas somehow. A chemical reaction, Captain said.

So we found Douglas grasping black plastic and bobbing barely afloat amid the debris, gulls swooping and shrieking excitement, and the sharks starting to stir in the distance, their fins cutting closer through the flotsam. It seems to bring everything to life, the dumping, contrary to what the critics say—we're feeding the seas. You've never seen so many fish surface, wallowing in the burbling sinkage, mouths gaping as if they'd swallow the bricks of crushed vegetable and rag waste whole. Gulls clamor and clap, delighted it seems, lighting on the barge decks to watch what comes rolling up: squared-off packs of compressed stuff the size of compact cars, which bob in the foam for a while as hundreds of gulls begin pecking, leaving each garbage block oozy and brilliant white with droppings, before the packs sink finally, carried off the continental shelf by outbound currents and to the seafloor some two thousand feet below, where they will sit for a million years, Captain says, until they are nothing but sand-covered slime.

We don't usually unload until we're three miles out, on the international sea, but sometimes Captain gets tired and lets it go early. He's got no patience with the tenderhearts who are making things hard nowadays, trying to ban sea dumps. Just like the people who eat steak, he says, but can't stand the thought of butchering and want their meat well done so they won't have to look at the blood. You got to take the heat if you're going to cook with fire, he says. They should be out here to feel what it's like. Tell us where to put a thirty-thousand-ton load. It's five barges long and Captain can barely pull it. We're four knots into the chop, the barges rolling on the wake like a flag in a breeze, the wash spilling up and over, our pumps working full-throttle, and a dark cloud of gulls a mile long spiraled behind like an airborne waterspout. Captain says we might go over night if the chop won't let up.

A night dump's something to see because some of this stuff glows. More chemical reaction, says Captain. Some of the fish glow too. Captain can't explain that but says it's just the way things are out here—you see all kinds of things people ashore can't figure. I was looking once to make sure the dump's going clear and suddenly a silver flash as big as a baseball diamond came up at me in the black water like a constellation falling from the sky. I toppled back and was nearly mauled by one of the lifters as it slammed into place. Just a school of fish, Captain told us, don't be scared, tenderhearts. He teases like that. But we do get scared sometimes. And Captain says smart people ought to. It's the only way to stay alive.

Here's trouble: the Canadian Coast Guard telling us over loudspeakers to back off, their huge red maple leaf flapping overhead as they arc around our bow, their uniformed young men at attention, squinting at us from the starboard side. They wear little caps that look like artist berets, every man clean-shaven and frowning at our smell, which the sun makes bigger than usual. You get used to it, tenderhearts! I shout at them, but they can't hear. Douglas turns to smile at me. It's a baby-like smile because he's got no teeth. Captain is cursing in the cabin. He sounds the horn, then starts talking to the Canadians over the radio, the static crackling like burning wood. If we let go here, they tell us, the stuff will find its way back to Newfoundland—they've got the currents figured out and there's no arguing with them because they've got guns and speed. Captain carries a rifle, shotgun, and two revolvers, enough for each of us, though we've never had reason to use them.

South we go, says Captain, steering that way. First Mate winches me and Douglas to the barges to make sure nothing comes loose as we make the course change. First Mate reminds us to wear our life vests, something we didn't start doing till Douglas went over that time. It does good to be unhampered by clothes back here, there's so much that gets in the way. So when it's real hot, life vests are all we wear, me and Douglas running along the rusted barge sides like Adam and Eve their first day, Paradise piled in steamy stacks before us and Nature clamoring all around. Douglas is what they call *dumb*, unable to speak anything but a grunt, so he's got a whistle around his neck he uses to signal me. Nobody can read him as well as I can, so Captain counts on my abilities when we need Douglas bad because Douglas is the one who does the dangerous stuff, dropping between two barges, say, to secure a chain when the chop could crush him like a cracker; or climbing up the barge tower in a thunderstorm to fix the antenna so we can call for help. I don't know where Captain got Douglas, but when I came on, his mate had just fallen dead from heart failure—an old man who'd been like a father to him—so Captain was looking for someone to bunk with Douglas and take the old man's place. I'm not that old, but I was willing to hold a head now and then and say, "There, now, it's not so bad," as Douglas bawled silently, his eyes awash but without a break of sound. I'd never seen anything like it.

Douglas enjoys running through the clouds of flies that hover always over the stacks. The birds give him a hard time because they think it's their territory; they swoop at him and even rain droppings. But Douglas doesn't mind. It's like he's one of them.

He whistles to let me know the pump on number three is out. He's standing on a stack, gulls circling over him, a cloud of flies like a black halo around his bald head. He has no body hair to speak of. Mutation, Captain calls it. Which means things didn't go right when his father and mother made him. But he's okay in the head. No one finds as many things wrong as he does—he can spot it immediately when a pump's out or a stack's giving way. I wave back to him to say I got the message, which I shout back to First Mate, who just shakes his head in disgust because he can't stand to see things go wrong the way things are starting to go today. First Mate's a young man who wanted to be in the U.S. Coast Guard but failed for some reason. Maybe because he couldn't stand to see things go wrong. It gets him twitchy, his right leg jittering like he's having spasms.

Douglas and I take off our clothes, it gets so hot, the barge mounds blasting furnace waves of odor, decomposing fast. We eat lunch under the barge tower on number five. Great thing about eating back here is that the flies and birds leave you alone, they have so much other stuff to pick at. Wave wash reaches where we sit, cooling the iron and making foam steam along the barge edge. Sitting out here's made us so dark we don't get blistered anymore. We got cans of chili and two handfuls of hard water biscuits for eats. Douglas tips his can to his mouth like drinking soda, the beans clinging to his upper lip and chin. When he's done he just tosses it overboard, and I wag a finger at him: Tenderhearts are going to sue you for that, Douglas.

He grins and gives me the finger.

A chopper overhead startles us because it seems to come from nowhere, dropping from the white-sunned sky like a monster bird about to settle on the tug and sink it. First Mate is shaking his fist at it. Douglas and I run up to see what's the matter. Turns out the state of Virginia is afraid we're going to let go nearby, which would foul the Chesapeake, so they're warning us off. It's like that all the way down the coast—two weeks and three refuels later.

First Mate says we ought to let go wherever we damn well please because these are international waters. But not international currents, Captain reminds him, smoothing a wrinkled hand over his gray beard. He looks at us like we have ideas. "Where are your clothes?" he asks. Douglas and I glance back to the barges and shrug. We forgot about them, we've been so busy, I tell him. Barge three is about to give in, so we've been trading pumps, moving four to three and back again. But it can't go on like that. We're exhausted. The wind's picked up so much the flies are clinging to the heaps like barnacles and the gulls waver overhead, fighting to keep up with us, their wings outstretched like stiff kite sails.

When the Florida Coast Guard speeds toward us, First Mate pulls Captain's shotgun from the rack and aims it out the cabin window. Douglas, on the outside, jumps up, pressing his forehead to the gun barrel, then he blows his whistle, startling First Mate so bad it gives Captain a chance to slam him with a cola bottle. By the time I get there they've got First Mate tied on the floor, Douglas sitting on his chest grinning and naked except for his orange life vest. It all happens so fast the young Coast Guard men don't see it—they're too serious to imagine such a thing, Captain says, every boy with narrowed eyes and pinched nose like we were some kind of floating plague. Go south, they tell us. So we do. But Captain's discouraged. Says he's getting too old for this kind of runaround. The city commission's going to hear about it. Things are getting too political, he says, glancing down at First Mate, who looks asleep, a welt the size of a hardball at the back of his head.

Douglas and I take turns holding ice on First Mate's head till he feels better. We spoon soup into his mouth but he lets half of it spill out, he's so angry. Let me go, he says over and over. Douglas shakes his head no and holds out another spoonful of chicken noodle. Eat, I tell him, or you'll get sick. He tells me to go to hell. We can't run the barges without him, he says, because Captain's too old to do the work of two men. Already pump four's starting to sputter with weakness, it's been moved and worked so much. One of the barges is going down. It's just a matter of time, says First Mate, glancing from me to Douglas and back again. Douglas shakes his head—no—once more. First Mate tells him to go to hell.

I winch Douglas to the barges so he can check the pumps. Captain's looking at charts and shaking his head. We may have to turn back, he says, though it might mean the end of his career. You just don't go out with thirty thousand tons and come back with it a month later. It costs a fortune. He's got to dump somewhere. First Mate says Mexico is the best bet. The whole country's a dump, he says. Captain tells me to take the wheel while he goes down for more charts. First Mate smiles up at me and says I'm the only one with brains on the boat. I'm the only one who's ever made sense in his thinking. After all, he says, who can understand Douglas best? And who does the Captain rely on when things get rough? I turn around to look at him. Me? I ask. Look who's at the wheel, he says: you. Let me go, he says, and I promise I'll behave. He speaks so kindly, I do what he says.

Then he punches me in the stomach, takes a pistol from Captain's drawer, and tells me to stand. Captain looks about to faint when he comes up and sees what's happened.

To Mexico, First Mate commands. He makes Captain pilot and he keeps the gun to my head, his right leg jittering. Douglas is whistling a warning that barge three's about to go. But I don't answer. When I glance back I see him standing on a stack and waving with both arms. But no one waves back. He's stuck out there now.

We'll drop our load into the gulf as soon as we can, First Mate says. The tug's slowing because barge three is filling with water. Douglas whistles frantically and the gulls shriek in response, they're so irritated. We'll all go down if

we don't do something about that barge, Captain tells First
Mate. Soon as it's dark, First Mate says, we're sinking the
barges. All of them. The whole thing will be logged as a
catastrophe. That way nobody will be to blame. What about
Douglas? I ask. First Mate shrugs. What about him? Suddenly we see an ocean liner, drifting like a white cloud on
the horizon, the first ship we've seen since leaving the city,
not counting flecks of sailboats in the distance now and
then. If we're going to log an accident, Captain says, we'll
have to signal distress. First Mate's eyes go wild with panic.
He shoots the radio. You shouldn't have done that, says Captain wearily.

Douglas whistles again. The gulls cry.

Something jerks the tug and we look back to see
barge three going down, garbage blocks beginning to float,
birds swooping madly, stirred by the change. Douglas is
behind with number four trying to unhook from the bow
cleat—he wants to save what he can. Captain groans. Untie! First Mate tells me, Untie! He shoves me to the back of
the tug. I'm on my knees staring at the froth churning from
the tug-end, chains clanking against the grease-streaked
stern, the blue-green water below. Captain cuts the engine.
First Mate jabs his pistol into my neck. The cold makes me
shiver. My hands grip for algae-covered chain links but
they're too slipperily and too heavy.

It takes two! I'm shouting, two people!

A jolt knocks First Mate down. Douglas has sent
load four over, emptying the barge, but the force of it,
dragged with sinking number three, makes the barge line
buckle. Now four is sinking and Douglas stands on five,
whistling for help. We're going down. I'm about to leap on
First Mate when Captain starts shooting, aiming for First
Mate, but missing, the bullets pinging off the deck. First
Mate dives. Then we follow.

The suck of sinkage pulls me down like a vacuum,
yanking off my life vest and spinning me like a corkscrew
until I'm so dizzy I don't know which is bottom and which
is top, my head and nose so full of stinging water it seems

my eyes will pop out. Pain inside and darkness everywhere. Confusion. Then there's light, a blinding glare on the water, so suddenly calm now. I spit up, blinking, reaching for something to save me—a clump of foam. Heaps all around burble as they sink, water bubbling and foaming, flies swirling in angry knots at the surface. I'm kneeing through, almost crawling, the dump load is so thick in the water. Captain dog-paddles toward me, his gray beard dripping, his eyes sad like a spaniel's. Follow me, he says. I'm panting, trying to call out for Douglas, but all I do is cough. The idea is to get as far from the junk as possible before the sharks come. Schools of fish flutter by, flashing in the turquoise below. There will be so much confusion, the sharks'll tear into whatever moves, tails flailing, fish darting frenzied through the dark passages of gnarled waste. Gulls watch us from sinking piles, their black eyes blinking as we paddle close by. They gobble strands of vegetable muck and snap at flies. A ship—the liner—sounds its horn, a distant moan. Does it see us?

How could it miss? Captain says.

What looks like a mound of oil-soaked fabric and foam just ahead is Douglas, we discover, dragging First Mate, who nearly drowned. Douglas smiles in greeting. I kiss his forehead. First Mate sputters, flailing in his savior's arms. He's as pale as fish belly. Captain says First Mate's going to jail as soon as we're picked up. All we have to do now is swim slow and easy until the liner sends out rescue. Expect an investigation, Captain says, and a lot of controversy.

Maybe we'll lose our jobs and be banned from the seas, he says. But that's something I can't imagine. Who's going to take out the trash? By the time we get back to the city another thirty thousand tons will be waiting for us, the people desperate to get rid of it, so I figure about this time next month we'll be at sea again, pulling another barge line and seeking another place to drop our load, me and Douglas working in the sun all day with the sea lapping our feet like nothing else exists except it, the stacks of garbage, and the endless horizon.

a Model Family

Mother bought us a submarine kit to build as a family project while our father is gone. It has 2,034 plastic pieces, seventeen decals, and ten feet of thread-like wire. It is a big model, the parts scattered all over our living room rug, and it comes with twenty-seven pages of instructions written in five different languages. We got the kit weeks ago but have not had time to start it because there are so many other things to work on around the house.

Father is on the nuclear submarine Zipperfish. He left six months ago. He and Mother argued about the trip, but he went anyway. He told me and Chip he was going on a secret mission. It sounds a little too adventuresome for my father, who is rather thin and studious, and I would not believe the story if my mother didn't have a picture to prove it. Father sent her a snapshot of him with the crew of the Zipperfish. Everyone is smiling with their arms around each other and everybody has a "flattop" haircut, the weirdest looking thing. My little brother Chip says they look like spacemen, and now he tells his friends that our father is on a secret mission somewhere near the moon.

Father is a civilian, an electrical engineer. Our basement is crowded with his old radios, television tubes, testing equipment (black boxes with glowing screens and eerie lights), and trays and trays of tiny parts, many of them colorful and oddly shaped like hard candy. When people ask me what my father does I tell them he fixes household appliances, which is no lie. He used to fix all our electrical stuff. Mother has a box in the kitchen closet where she keeps the broken appliances for his return. She bought a do-it-yourself handyman's book, which she reads little by little each day, but she has not tried to fix anything since she blew the fuses while working on the blender. The house was dark for hours and we wandered around the living room crunching model pieces underfoot, waiting for Mr. Kiminski, a retired handyman who lives down the street.

Mr. Kiminski wants to take me and Chip hunting, but we do not want to go because he scares us. He looks like one of those sickly Santas we see in front of Saint Mary's Halfway House every year. He has piggish eyes and a short white beard stained brown and yellow. He looks like maybe he knows Chip and I used to pee on his prize geraniums.

After he fixed our fuse box, Mother invited him to dinner. He got upset when Chip told him he wanted to be a witch for Halloween.

"Witches are girls," said Mr. Kiminski, like saying *the sky is blue, everybody knows.*

"Witches are monsters," said Chip. He offered his good-boy smile, then dropped a pat of butter into his steamy mashed potatoes.

"You want a *dress*, then," said the old man.

"Is that what you want, Chip, a dress?" Mother asked.

It sounded like we were asking him, *Scabs, Chip, you want to eat scabs?*

"I want to be a witch." Chip shrugged. What was so hard to understand? "A witch with a ugly green face and horrible thoughts." He tore the center out of his bread and squeezed it into a doughy ball.

Shaking his head sadly, Mr. Kiminski sighed. "These boys need a strong hand."

Chip asked if that meant we were going to get spanked.

"You're going hunting," Mr. Kiminski announced.

"You're going to learn to live like men."

"They're young, Mr. Kiminski." Mother smiled at us.

"You'll have young pansies if you're not careful." He eyed us suspiciously.

Pansies, I was pretty sure, are flowers. And I thought again of the old man's prize geraniums.

Kiminiski leaned toward us, almost smiling, like he was about to share a dirty secret. "You boys ever shoot a deer?"

The way he said this made my face burn because I could not understand why he would be so happy about shooting a deer.

Chip began to blubber, whining about Bambi, a movie he had seen recently. Tears dripped all over his plate.

"Mr. Kiminski." Mother's cheeks were red—maybe like mine, I thought. "These are not your boys to browbeat."

"They need help," he said. He sounded angry now.

Mother told Kiminski to leave. He said she was a frustrated woman who needed a little looking after. She grabbed a greasy spatula and told him to leave now or regret the consequences. He pinched my cheek and promised to take me and Chip hunting real soon. After he left, Chip and Mother cried for a long time. I was feeling pretty sad myself, so I walked down to Kiminski's and poured turpentine all over his flowers.

Mother says Chip and I are losing our discipline, so she makes Chip take art lessons and she makes me go to speech therapy. I stutter a lot and it nearly drives her crazy, it takes me so long to answer her questions. At school I am in speech class while the rest of the kids are in study hall where most of the note passing occurs. I miss out on vital developments in our sixth grade social life and it really hurts my image.

I try to make up for this on Wednesday afternoons, when I take Chip on the train to the city for his art lessons. While I wait for him in the park, I practice at picking up girls. I am not that interested in girls, really, but it seems like the thing to do, so I want to be good at it. I have tried several approaches but have found that I get the best response if I wave my arms and moan like a deaf-mute: people seem to want to help. Still, the pretty girls ignore me. They go for those hotshot skateboarders who race around at startling speeds, pirouetting left and right and wheeling backwards on one leg. Guys like that have no regard for personal safety. That's why the girls love them.

My mother would not buy me a skateboard even if I begged her. Recently, though, she offered to get me some roller skates. I haven't told her that I am scared of spinning around on tiny wheels like that. My father was a fine ice skater when he was young, she tells me, and someday, if I practice, I can wear his skates, which are in the attic—battered black leather things with rusted runners.

Mother met Father while ice skating. It was a long time ago, she says, when he was in the Navy. She says he looked like a gypsy in his dark blue uniform.

"I was a stupid eighteen-year-old," she says. "Just out of high school, a piccolo player in the marching band. My parents were glad to see me go. They had ten kids. It was all they could do just to keep track of us, much less teach us anything important like how to cook. But your father was patient. He got what he wanted."

"Ice skates?" I ask.

"A pretty wife," she says. She pours me a glass of milk, then pours a little into her steaming tea.

I stutter. "You were pretty?"

"I was a prize," she says. She sits in front of her teacup and almost looks happy. "I got plenty of attention. I used to enter beauty contests."

"Chip and I give you plenty of attention."

"Sometimes too much," she says. She smiles into her tea, like there might be a mystery there.

"I guess we spoil you," I insist.

"That's right." She looks at me finally, and I am relieved to see her smile again. "You two spoil me."

Chip pretends our father has been gone for years instead of months, and sometimes he imagines him as a hero from television. One week our father is Superman and the next week he is The Hulk. Chip is six, old enough to know better, and Mother gets angry when she hears him describing Father as "a big green guy with size fifty biceps and teeth as big as piano keys."

She grabs Chip's collar and says, "Your father is six feet tall, his hair is black, his eyes are brown, his teeth are *normal* because he brushes them three times a day, he is clean-shaven, has a large nose like your brother, and for better or worse he is the man half responsible for you two clowns, and I don't want to hear him described in any peculiar fashion. Understand?"

Chip nods yes, then continues watching television, which is about all he does besides his art lessons. His art teacher wants him to be a landscape painter. She says he has great line control. Chip paints pages and pages of lines for her. Mother claims it takes discipline to paint so many straight lines. I say it's a sign of stupidity.

What Chip lacks in sophistication he makes up for in charm. He has that wholesome kind of freckled face you see on cereal commercials. Women love him. Just now, for instance, an old lady gave him a dollar for picking up her gloves from the floor of the train station. Chip was down there pretending he was a turtle. I have to watch over him all the time, he's so childish. His sneakers are wet from the snow because he forgot to wear his galoshes, and his nose is dripping all over the place. I make him sit down and we take turns drawing pictures on the foggy train window.

"Last night I dreamed we built a snowman," he says. "And when it melted it turned into Dad."

"Fascinating," I say.

"Maybe we ought to try it," he says.

"Maybe you ought to grow up," I tell him.

"It might work. That kind of thing happens all the time on TV." He is carefully fingering a snowman's face: big eyes and a stitch of a mouth.

"Dad is not like one of your television heroes. Why should you want to see him?" I am drawing a rocket ship.

"He took us to the amusement park once."

"Twice," I say, "but you were too young to remember."

"I remember everything." He pauses to wipe his nose on his coat sleeve. "Even the time we went to Africa."

"That was the zoo."

"We were nearly eaten by headhunters, but Dad fought them off." He draws clouds smoking from the end of my rocket ship.

"It was at the zoo," I tell him in a you're-so-stupid voice. "A little monkey grabbed your pant leg, and Dad slapped the monkey's wrist."

"You make up such stories," he says, his finger poised for more drawing.

"You're lucky to have me around, buddy."

"I'm honored," he says, twirling his finger. "I'm truly honored." Then he draws a goofy face on the window and writes my name under it.

The city station is large and old like a museum and thousands of people are rushing back and forth, everyone with a destination. Their voices echo around the dome of the lobby. Chip and I stop at a newsstand to buy a week's supply of bubble gum. Mother lets us chew only the sugarless kind, so we have to sneak in the normal stuff. Chip makes a point of cramming as many pieces as possible into his mouth. It takes him a long time to chew them down into a manageable wad.

I am reading my gum wrapper comic when I hear my father's voice giving someone directions not far behind me. His voice is not loud, but it is a different color than the rest and it reaches me clearly above the others. I see his shoulders from the back and I know it is him because he walks like no other man. For a moment I am dizzy, like I have just stumbled and found, right there in the grass at my feet, a big bar of gold that will buy us a penthouse and a big screen TV and make all of us very happy for the rest of our lives.

I shout for my father to stop—*He's right there,* I tell myself, *he will turn around.* I shout, "Hey, Dad, wait!" But, strangely, he does not seem to hear. I pull Chip with me and run after him. Chip yells and complains because he does not know what is happening. I shout again for Father, who is lost in the crowd, and people turn from all sides to stare at me like I'm crazy. In my mind I am watching the whole thing on a movie screen, I feel so far away.

Chip and I run outside in time to see Father enter a taxi. He glances back for a second and almost sees us before the cab disappears in traffic.

Chip shakes himself from my grip. "What's your problem?" he says.

"Dad was right here and he didn't see us. Like a ghost or something."

Chip thinks I am pulling his leg. He rolls his eyes and blows a bubble.

"You just saw him drive away, Chip!"

"I saw you lose your marbles."

"Okay, he was different. He had a mustache and his hair was longer, but it was Dad. You can't mistake a thing like that."

"Father is on a spaceship exploring the galaxy." Chip makes rocket noises.

"You're crazy." I push him away. "You don't care. You just make jokes."

"Sure I care," he says. "I'm missing my art lesson."

"Maybe he was in disguise. Maybe this is part of his secret mission."

"You want a pretzel?" Chip buys a hot pretzel from a vendor and tears it in half. "These things make great nose warmers." He sticks his small nose into the steamy dough of a pretzel half.

"I almost blew his cover," I realize. "I almost gave him away."

"Dad will be back soon enough. Don't worry."

"Blow your nose," I tell him. "It's dripping all over."

"It's so cold I can't tell," he says. "Do I have icicles?"

"We cannot let Mother know."

"She doesn't mind if my nose drips a little."

"About Dad. We can't let her know about Dad in disguise."

"It was a good disguise," says Chip, offering me his dopey smile. "It sure had me fooled."

We arrive home just as it starts raining. Mother is cleaning up after her bridge party. The house is foggy with cigarette smoke, and the candy dishes are half filled with chocolate-covered raisins and nuts which Chip and I eat as fast as we can before Mother tries to put them away. Chip starts to tell her how I went crazy at the train station this afternoon, but I tackle him and push him under the couch to keep him quiet. He kicks and yells.

"What's with you boys?" she says.

"Chip's been making up stories all day," I tell her.

"Let me out," Chip says.

"Enough of this nonsense," says Mother. "What kind of TV dinner do you boys want?" She holds up four frozen choices.

"Spaghetti," says Chip from under the couch. I choose chicken.

Chip places the plastic trays inside the microwave, then he sets the timer. "I'm a good cook," he says.

I tell him he's a cooked goose if he opens his mouth again.

After dinner, Mother suggests we start on the submarine model. She says she will give us a big prize if we finish it before Father comes home. Since we do not know when that will be, we'll have to work fast. The model pieces are scattered like the remains of an explosion. We rake them into a big pile, and Mother reads the instructions to us by the light of the television set. She says the finished model will be in two halves showing each side of the sub's interior with working parts and a crew of tiny plastic men. Chip glues the tiny men into a clump so they will not get lost. Mother makes him unglue them. I work on the torpedo room. Chip starts on the periscope, but he loses interest when the space warriors on TV have a shootout. Mother works on the engine room, but soon she falls asleep with her head on the book of instructions and a tube of glue in her hands. Chip and I cover her with a throw rug, then we search the house for more candy she might have hidden for future bridge games. We find none.

All night it rains and hails, clattering on the roof, and this morning everything is glazed with ice: ice on telephone lines, ice on doghouses, ice on bushes and trees, ice on the basketball in our front yard.

"There are skaters in the street!" says Chip, bounding down the stairs.

"What does it mean?" I ask.

"Breakfast," says Mother from the kitchen.

Chip slings his ice skates over the back of his chair. "Everything is covered with rock candy." He runs to the bay window in the living room. "This is a special day like in my dreams."

"No school today." I spoon brown sugar over my oatmeal.

"Plenty of time to shovel the driveway," says Mother.

"It's Dad!" says Chip. "It's Dad coming home!"

Mother drops her spoon and hurries to the window. "Where?"

I step between them and lean on the windowsill. "Some guy skating up the street," I tell her. "It could be anybody, he's so far away."

"He skates just like Dad," says Chip.

"Yes, he does." Mother is squinting. "Sort of."

"Now we can all go skating together."

Mother leans closer to the window. She stands very still, her lips parted slightly as if she's trying to remember something from long ago. "We don't know for sure," she says finally.

"It's him," says Chip. "He's back." He dances around like a leprechaun.

"He would've called," Mother tells us.

"The telephone lines are down," I say.

"Maybe he didn't have his calling card," says Chip.

"Where's the telescope?" she says. "Get the telescope."

Chip runs into the den and returns with a small, colorfully painted telescope. "From my pirate's chest," he says.

Mother holds the telescope to her right eye and twists the focus ring. The skater is wearing a navy blue overcoat and bell-bottom trousers and a red scarf, which flutters from his neck. He leans from side to side as he pushes forward, skating nearer.

"Is he carrying presents?"

"Does he have a mustache?" I ask her. "Or a flattop haircut?"

"Should we wave?"

"He has a beard," says Mother.

"He's been away a long time," says Chip.

"He looks unhappy." Mother refocuses.

"It's dark and lonely in those little submarines."

"Oh my god," she says, "it's Mr. Kiminski."

"Mr. Kiminski!"

"Old man Kiminski skating this way." She drops the telescope and it falls on Chip's left foot. "How can I be so stupid, listening to you kids?" She returns to the kitchen.

Chip squints through the telescope. "Jeesh," he says, "it's Mr. Kiminski."

"You boys finish your breakfast."

Chip tosses the telescope onto the couch. "I've lost my appetite."

"You've lost your discipline," she says. "You're high strung and overimaginative, and I don't know what I'm going to do with you."

"Sell me at the flea market," says Chip.

"Get in here and eat your oatmeal." She is angry and Chip obeys.

I stand at the window and watch Mr. Kiminski skate to our house. He takes his time because he knows we are not going anywhere. Perhaps he has known all along that our father has been in the city and never on a submarine, that our father has been growing a mustache and longer hair and leading a different life for reasons I can only imagine.

Kiminski puffs great clouds of fog as he struggles up our drive. He slips and falls into the snowy yard, but regains his balance after many minutes of maneuvering. He pauses to catch his breath, panting, then he tries to kick the frozen basketball out of his way. He falls again and curses, swiping the air this way and that. I wonder why he takes the trouble to come here where he knows he is not welcome. He shuffles on his hands and knees like a seal and clambers finally onto the front steps. The bell rings and none of us moves for the door. We will sit at the breakfast table and pretend Father is here to answer it.

Loaves and Fishes

I n the last months of fighting, the bombing of our
Capital grew so consistent that it became as famil-
iar in our lives as the tolling of Saint Alice's church bells
two blocks away, though we hadn't heard the bells recently,
since they'd been taken for scrap. Usually, the first mortar
round started at three in the afternoon and the last ended
at six-thirty. Rumor had it that the RM or the PM—nobody
knew who was bombing whom—had to wait until three
because, by that time, their cannons were thawed and their
ammunition was dry finally. The rain was the worst it'd
been in memory. It might have seemed more tolerable had
it been snow. But we were in that indecisive half-season
between winter and spring, with freezes at night and heavy
drizzle all day.

Whenever the ground thawed, usually about noon,
all manner of debris would rise from the mud. One morning a half-rotted, rose-patterned, gingham-upholstered
loveseat rose from our neighbor's rear yard; from another
yard blossomed the many-colored necks of fifty-nine glass
beer bottles at least a half-century old; and from the dirt
floor of one neighbor's basement erupted a galvanized steel
wash basin, like new except for a fist-sized hole in the bottom. Before the Revolutionary Militia scrap collectors could
confiscate the find, the lucky family rushed the basin to the

nearest scrapper, who gave them, in exchange, two weeks' ration of cheese-food concentrate, a quart of milk substitute, and five pounds of National Toffee.

Some insisted that the bombing was the cause of the recent upheavals. Others said it was simply the earth disgorging a surfeit of human refuse. Still others said it— the rain which was drowning our part of the world—was a clear sign of global warming. The future, they insisted, would be a very wet one, and we would have to devolve to our earlier gilled selves or perish.

Whatever the cause, and irrespective of our fate, the one indisputable fact, we all agreed, was that we in the newer parts of the city were living on a forgotten landfill. And everything was coming up. That old song lyric, "Everything's coming up roses," kept going through my head as I stood at the rear window—now covered over with plastic, the glass long shattered—and watched my thirteen children, barefoot and oblivious to the chill, stamping and prodding our rear yard every afternoon. They were convinced that we were sitting on something big.

"Otherwise why wouldn't some of the smaller stuff, like television sets and exercycles, have come up?" asked Lori, my pragmatic one.

To tell the truth, as long as the children stayed busy, stayed away from trouble, and stayed nearby, I was happy to have them out of the flat, because I was trying to finish the rebuild of an old 586 PC in the workshop Marcel and I shared. Where was Marcel? On the front, I'd heard. And I wanted to hear no more. The frontier was the worst of the fighting because it was complicated by murderous ethnic bands who populated the mountains.

The old 586 would be a homecoming present. By the time it was done, I told myself, Marcel would be back. But, cowardly, I was taking my time. Some mornings I'd just stare at the empty monitor screen and imagine it was a crystal ball. Show me a better world, I'd demand of it. Show me my husband happy and home. Show me my foolish son, Lofe, hasn't become a killer.

Lofe had joined the Revolutionary Militia shortly after Marcel was drafted. I was so angry at this, I shouted after Lofe, "Take your brothers and sisters with you—you can use them as targets!" Lofe glanced back with a perplexed expression, as if to say, Why would you want to talk like that?

Sad to say, he was far from my brightest child.

I tried not to feel sorry for myself. Every family had hardships, and some had already received the remains of loved ones in small aluminum boxes. Whenever an RM courier biked down our cratered street, you could hear doors slamming one after the other, like dominoes falling.

"Come see what we found!" Simon announced, startling me at my work.

"Knock before entering," I said.

"Can't do that," he said, "we used up the door."

For firewood. There wasn't a door left in the place.

"What'd you find?" I asked warily. Last week they had dug up the water pipes and would have torn them out had I not stopped them. We were still getting water one hour every other day.

"Come see!"

Our rear yard was like a hundred others on either side of us, a narrow stretch of dirt—now mud—between two shoulder-high brick walls and, at the back, a chain-link gate into the alley. The gate had been stolen for scrap months ago.

The children were dancing muddy circles in the drizzle. My little tribe of savages. Celebrating what? At first glance, the thing in their midst looked like a muddy slab of yellowish concrete. Slowly the drizzle was washing it clean. I was surprised to discover that this was the rear end of a large American automobile. A Buick Delta 88, the chrome lettering said. It had a nice pale gold paint job, the trunk large enough to carry an upright piano, the formidable bumper all of chrome, and the taillights—of red glass!—were intact.

"It's a car!" the children squealed. "It's a car!"

"Not so loud!" I hushed them. There was enough metal here to keep us eating well for a year at least.

"Let's take it to the scrapper!" Nadia said.

"How?" I asked. Three quarters of the car was still buried—but rising slowly, I suspected. "We'll have to wait."

"We could winch it out," said Lori. She had my mathematical mind.

"We have nothing for leverage," I said.

"We leave it here too long, somebody's going to find it."

The little ones were patting the thing as if it were a behemoth pet.

"Block up the gate," I said.

"The gate!" the children echoed in panic. Soon they had piled pieces of plaster, chunks of asphalt, broken brick and concrete in the gate-space so that only the tallest passerby would have been able to peer into our muddy yard. And why would anyone bother?

"Let's take it apart!" one of the children said.

"It's not that easy." I was sizing up the thing, all that steel. We had no acetylene torch, no pry bars, no hacksaws, no sledgehammers, no chisels.

"Bomb coming," said Redding.

"A screaming Mimi," said Sara.

Now I heard the whistling. "Everybody inside," I said. They moaned in disappointment. "And wipe your feet."

The first Mimi hit about a quarter mile away. A Mimi's impact always made a disappointing *pop* like the clap of two large hands. Many of them didn't even explode. That seemed to speak generally for the war effort on both sides.

When I got into the flat, I found the children gathered around a stranger in our front room.

"Who're you?" they were chattering. "You got candy?" They were grasping at her uniform—she was an RM courier, I could tell by the blue star on her bicycle helmet. She wore a tartan plaid kilt, muddy white blouse, calf-high cowboy boots, also very muddy, and a sash that said, in satin letters, "Capital City Boots!" Which meant that the Revolutionary Militia had succeeded in capturing Capital City High School, one of the Presidential Militia's strongholds. The CC Boots had been the school's competitive dance squad.

Ignoring the children, she said, "I got a call for you if you want to take it." In one hand she held out her pocket phone. She couldn't have been more than sixteen or seventeen, a girl with a milky complexion, stunning blue eyes—like a malamute's—and orange hair.

"A call for me?" I said idiotically. The Mimies were falling steadily now; I heard their pop-pops to the left, to the right, especially close today. The call, I supposed, was from the RM Home Base, some demand I could hardly fulfill. Or, worse, news that Marcel or Lofe was dead.

"Go on," the girl insisted, her expression letting me know that it wasn't so bad. "Take it."

The children had unfastened her sash and were parading around the room with it.

"Into the basement," I told them. "Now."

"You heard your mother," the courier said. "Let's go."

I was impressed, and a little chagrined, that the children listened to her. She shepherded them away. "No running," she called.

"What do you need?" I said into the phone.

"Mama, I'm a sergeant!"

"Lofe?" My son, his reedy voice unmistakable! I pictured him at a kiosk near the park, sun on his face, flowers blooming at his feet. But, of course, this was ridiculous. "Where are you?"

"In the Capital, Mama."

"I assumed that much, Lofe. *Where* in the city?"

"Not far from the President's House—I just wanted to let you know you don't have to worry anymore. The revolution has triumphed!" Mouthing the party line.

"The war's hardly over, Lofe. Don't you hear the bombs?"

He was silent for a moment, maybe listening to the Mimies. "Yeah, there's some bombing."

"Are you all right, my little turtle?"

"Mama, the phones are tapped—they're going to laugh at me."

"How can the war be over and the fighting continue?"

"I guess some people don't understand what's happened."

"You're not fighting, are you?"

"Not now," he said. Such a simple boy.

"Lofe, come home."

"I've got a career in the RM," he said. "They just gave me a new uniform."

"A kilt and cowboy boots?"

Again he paused. "You've seen it?"

I was hoping to ignite some childhood superstition, that a parent is omniscient. "There's very little that I don't know, Lofe. And one thing I know for certain is that the war isn't over."

"We call it the Revolution," he corrected.

"Whatever you want to call it, it's not over."

As if to punctuate my pronouncement, a Mimi streaked overhead then exploded with a crack a block away.

"I just wanted to let you know," he said.

Let me know he was still alive.

"Come home, my little turtle."

"Mama."

"Your brothers and sisters keep asking after you."

"Mama."

He was on the verge of tears.

"Last night baby Tori said—"

The line went dead. It was tapped, I remembered him saying. I stared at the phone in my hand, willed it to ring. The walls of our building shuddered under the Mimi assault, plaster dust drifting over me like fog.

I might have stood there for the rest of the afternoon, staring at that phone and fighting back my tears, had

Officer Hermes, the RM scrap collector, not come to the door—or what served as a door, a patchwork of stapled plastic, which he rattled politely. Since his several recent heart attacks, Hermes had been a changed man, much easier-going and sometimes downright stupid. He shouldn't have been out during the air raid, for instance.

"Stopped by to see what you had for me," he said with a small bow, nearly shouting to be heard over the bombing.

"Let me get you something," I said. Considering his heart condition, he was a startlingly young man, not more than twenty-two, with a cherubic, downy face. He wore a uniform made of an assortment of tacked-together rags and a kitchen pot for a helmet, his feet wrapped in silver duct tape. Quite a comedown for a man who used to be the best dressed in the eastern ward—in the days he was getting kickbacks.

To tell the truth, I felt sorry for him and was certain he would meet an unfortunate end.

"How about these?" I asked, handing him a stack of old cassette tapes. "Melt them down and make something."

He was nodding agreeably. "I'll melt them down and make something."

"Goodbye," I said, guiding him back to the door. "Watch out for the bombs."

"There's good metal in bombs," he said.

"I wouldn't mess with them if I were you."

He gave a final nod, then stepped back into the drizzle which, as it hit the top of his pot-helmet, in the silence between bomb-falls, sounded like the spit-crackle of frying pork rind. Slung over his left shoulder, he carried a bag weighted with his many collections, probably most of it useless like the cassette tapes.

Downstairs, I found the children and the courier sitting two to a step and staring into the basement—which was, I discovered, filled with black water.

"It's about three feet deep," the courier announced.

"It's really cold," said one of the children.

"We don't have to worry about the water pipes now."

"Plenty to drink."

"What's all that junk?" I said.

"Landfill," said Lori matter-of-factly.

Pottery fragments, plastic bottles, a few rubber doll heads bobbing like fish-floats, beads, rag-bits, plastic tubing, snakes of rope, and brown-green amoebic wads of ancient cardboard.

The floating mess made me think of drowned children. Most of mine didn't know how to swim. "Upstairs," I told them.

"We'll get bombed," one of them protested.

I sighed. "To tell the truth, my babies, it doesn't matter where we are if a bomb hits us."

Nadia said, "Thanks for being so gloomy, Mama."

I *had* grown gloomy, hadn't I? If—when—Marcel came home, he wouldn't know me, I feared. Or he simply wouldn't care for me, a woman who had gotten old and bitter in his absence. Like the broad streak of gray in my hair, my pessimism seemed to have appeared overnight.

I had promised myself years ago that I would never regret forgoing a degree in higher mathematics for the large family Marcel had wanted so badly, but here I was, surrounded by children and bombs and mud, and what did I have to show for all my efforts? My children were wearing shower curtains for clothes; there were no windows in the house, no doors, not even faucet handles; and our greatest thrill after two years of war was to find, rising from our soupy backyard, a large American automobile. Who wouldn't be bitter?

Upstairs, Officer Hermes had returned. He was going through my kitchen drawers, looking for silverware, most of which I kept hidden under the sink.

When he saw me he said, "Oops," with his usual bow and a sheepish smile, "you caught me." Hastily he closed the rag-filled drawer he'd been rummaging through. "My quota's real low. I haven't been doing well with metals."

"It's Hermes the Heart Attack!" the children were taunting. They had seen him collapse a number of times; in fact, once I had to revive him myself with CPR.

"Shame on you, Officer Hermes," I said. "Children, hush."

Our young courier took two steps toward Hermes and said, as if scolding a dog, "I could have you arrested here and now, mister."

"But *I'm* a government official," Hermes protested. Panicked, he fumbled in his ratty pocket for his plastic ID card.

"Conduct most unbecoming," I said with disgust. Though I had no intention of reporting him, I wanted him to squirm a little. I turned to the courier. "Don't you think, miss?"

"Her name's Cassandra," Lori announced.

"Cassandra?" I smiled at the young woman. "Doomed to see a future no one believes?"

She blinked twice, confused, embarrassed. "Beg your pardon?"

"Your name," I said. Now I felt embarrassed. Didn't anyone understand anything?

"My mother named me after my great aunt," Cassandra explained.

Too young, I thought: they're all too young. What did they teach in school nowadays?

Hermes, with trembling hand, held out his ID tag. "I haven't been doing well on my quota. For some reason I keep bringing in plastic. They don't want plastic, they want metal. But I keep bringing in plastic. I can't think straight— it's my heart, you know, it makes me think crooked."

A couple of the children said, "Don't cry, Hermes." Their sympathy was gratifying, if a little undermined by a few giggles from the children behind me.

"My bike!" Cassandra gasped. Talk of metal must have triggered her memory: had she forgotten to secure her bike?

The children stormed after her to the front door.

Hermes looked at me with wide eyes: "I didn't take it!"

"Gone!" I heard the courier wail from the stoop. "Somebody stole my bike!"

Hermes and I went to her. She was shaking her head in disbelief, her face pale from shock—you could be a courier only if you had your own bicycle; nobody, not even the new government, had a bike to loan you. I felt especially bad for Cassandra because it seemed my family was at fault—we had distracted her, hadn't we?

The children moaned in sympathy and clutched at her hands. "We'll get it back!" "We'll get another bike!" "We'll build you a bike!"

"I'm done for," she said. "They'll fire me."

Just then the phone in my back pocket—Cassandra's phone—rang. I handed it to her. "What do you want?" she barked into the thing.

She listened. A Mimi whistled overhead. I waited for the explosion but it didn't come.

"I'm pinned down by bombing," Cassandra told the phone finally.

The children shouted, "Boom! Boom!"

I hushed them.

Cassandra slapped her phone shut, then dropped it into the pouch at the front of her kilt. "They want me to make another run."

"Stay here with us," I said. "You can help dismantle the car—we'll give you enough to buy a used bike."

"Car?" Hermes said.

I turned to him. "You can have some too, Officer."

"Metal?" he asked. "You'll give me some metal?"

There was enough for everyone, wasn't there?

One small objection tried to surface from the mud of my thoughts: shouldn't I have held the car, *in toto,* for my family? Didn't I owe them my fiercest parsimony?

I looked from Hermes, who gaped at me like a hungry dog, to Cassandra, who regarded me with narrowed eyes and a skeptical smirk, then to the children, who were hopping in place, waving their hands, shouting, "We're gonna get the car!" And I decided that only the grandest gesture would do.

It took no more than an hour to assemble my many neighbors. They stood ankle-deep or deeper in mud, laying their hands on the Delta 88's tawny-colored metal, stroking it, tugging at it. "The silvery metal's called chrome." "That's still good rubber on the tires—you could make shoes of it." "They don't put glass like this in Minotaurs, see how thick?" "The backseat's as big as a bed."

I ordered fat Mr. Leo, who used to be a pastry chef at the National Hotel, to serve as our anchor. Five of us hoisted him to the rear bumper, where he dangled for a moment while the rest of us—about twenty in number— jumped for a handhold. At that moment, a Mimi hit the house, scalping the roof, shingles flying, the top half of the rear wall falling in. The bomb flew straight through to the other side, exploding in the street with a rumble that I felt to the tips of my fingers.

That's when the car came free, the rear dropping into the mud and the nose bobbing up, the whole thing wallowing like a beached orca. We were on it immediately, clambering over the trunk and roof. The children joined us. It seemed we might sink, every one of us, into the muck, but the car stabilized finally.

I didn't think about our ruined flat and I hardly considered how we might have been maimed or killed had we been inside. I thought about only this miraculous find of metal, which we were now pounding on and tearing at. A feeding frenzy. Mr. Leo, with his considerable weight, managed to wrench off the rear trunk lid. Tanya, from a few houses down, had a screw driver and was deftly dismantling the taillights. My children had already peeled away the chrome trim. I imagined a tribe of Aleuts dismantling a whale, picking it clean to the bone, every string of gristle, every handful of fat, put to good use.

The hole from which the car had risen was already filled with mud, our rear yard a black morass of muck and landfill debris—it was the garbage, the lumpy flotsam, that was keeping us from sinking.

It was nearly midnight, and well past curfew, by the time we got the car dismantled to the chassis. One hundred sixty-three neighbors got a piece of the Delta 88: they carried away rear-view mirrors, door handles, latches, lids, fenders, trim, light cowls, windowpanes, wipers, and slabs of metal the size of place mats—someone had brought a gas-powered coping saw. I was surprised, though I shouldn't have been, by the many tools my neighbors had been hoarding. I gave the front bonnet, the hood, to Officer Hermes, who could drag it no farther than down the block a few doors where, exhausted and mud-covered, he promptly went to sleep, cradled in the lid and covered, like a corpse, with a yellow plastic poncho.

Cassandra helped me put my muddy children to bed in what remained of our flat. We lined them up, one beside the other, down the hallway, covering as many as we could with carpet from the dismantled car. Some of them shared armrests as pillows. At their feet was our family trophy, the Delta's front grill, which looked like an ornate chrome gate. The rust was hardly noticeable.

Cassandra herself got the rear bumper and the tire jack.

"You think that'll be enough?" I asked her.

"Maybe," she said. "You've been more than generous."

Had I really? The car was hardly mine to give away.

"I was lucky," I said. "And you were unlucky."

"Or lucky enough to have lost my bike here," she said. "I worry about the penalties you may incur."

"What can they do to us?" I said. "There's nothing left to take."

At this I felt my bitterness resurface. I was so angry but did not know where to direct it: at the soldiers? the bureaucrats? the lackeys like Hermes? the citizenry in general? my many neighbors who, since the shortages began, I hadn't heard one word from? myself for putting up with this?

"I hope to see you again," Cassandra said.

Will you see me again? I wanted to ask her. Tell me the future, Cassandra.

We shook hands. I kissed her on each cheek. Then she hefted the bumper onto her right shoulder and walked into the cold night. The drizzle had turned to a fine snow.

When I returned to the back of the flat, where the rear door's plastic drop sheet rattled in the breeze, I expected to see the Delta 88 chassis, with its black block of an engine, gone, sunk again deep into the mud. But it remained, now white with snow, a huge skeleton. The next day, the RM scrap collectors towed it away after much work. No questions asked.

Years later, after the war was over, I still saw pieces of the old car around our ward: roof shingles cut from its chassis; taillights used as planters; the thick blue-tinted windows sliced into small replacement panes; aluminum trim used as window flashing; chromed dashboard knobs strung as fashionable pendants; the steering wheel as the base of a floor fan. I myself used its chromed hubcaps as soup bowls. Even after I finally replaced them with cheap ceramic bowls from the new RM Co-op, I refused to let them go because, despite the bitter memories they sometimes gave rise to, I liked their shine.

Ruth

After moving in with Ruth, he didn't know what to do with himself. He had been a drummer on the casino circuit for nineteen years, playing third-rate rooms in cowtowns like Elko, Winnemuca, and worse, and when he stopped finally it seemed his hands no longer belonged to him—they just sat like useless pets in his lap, too good for other work. So he drank a lot of beer and watched TV (Ruth had cable) or, when TV got tiresome, he stared out at the Sierra Nevadas, whose blue peaks he could see from Ruth's bedroom window if he positioned her oak rocker just right.

He grew a beard. He gained twenty pounds. Ruth said he was getting to look like a lumberjack. So, after one month of this "vacationing," as she called it, she got him a job at a donut house on the Strip, though he didn't really want it. The only good thing about the job was the hours, midnight till dawn, which he was used to because they were musician's hours. He was given a white smock and a chef's hat and told to "guard the nuts," which meant he had to stand at the fry trough all night and watch the rings of dough browning in hot oil. At dawn, he'd come home exhausted and stinking of burnt grease. He didn't last long at it, though, because one night, after drinking a six pack during break, he started deep-frying plastic napkin holders, watching them melt like cheese.

Ruth was worried about him. She said, "You're having a midlife crisis and you don't know it." He was only thirty-eight, but he figured maybe she was right, she was so much smarter than he. Ruth dealt blackjack at the Hilton, where she worked the graveyard shift. She'd been dealing in Reno for more than twenty years, though she never said how many more exactly. She was older than he was and he liked that, because she was so reliable and steady, not at all like the women he'd met on the road. Those women, the ones who messed with musicians, were never looking for much, he'd learned, because musicians are like truckdrivers, always going where the work takes them. You couldn't get serious about somebody who was just passing through the way Erik had passed through nearly every town in Nevada.

He'd got his first pair of drumsticks when he was twelve, in 1970, when rock and roll was happening big. Every other boy he knew in sixth grade was taking drums, carrying their sticks all day to mark their difference from the unmusical others and practicing their rudiments on the blacktop at recess while the rest were playing kickball. But only Erik was really good at it. It was the first time he had excelled at anything, and he was grateful for the gift. That's what it was, his mother told him, a gift.

His parents bought him a drum kit; they didn't mind him practicing every evening in the basement, because he was a good boy and undistinguished in everything but his drumming. He made the school dance band and, at the end-of-the-year dance, he got to beat a solo on the last number, the girls and boys crowding around, their eyes gleaming with what looked like envy as he splashed cymbals and boomed toms, the drum riser shuddering from the force of his attack. A few of the prettiest girls stayed after to watch him pack up and to ask questions that weren't really questions. Don't you get tired playing fast like that? Isn't it scary to play all alone? And later, as he wheeled his trap case out, some of the coolest guys turned to him in the hall and flashed the peace sign. They said, "Far out, Erik. It was far out. . . ." He felt like a stunt pilot after an airshow.

There had been a time when he believed he'd work his way out of the casino circuit and into something better, like studio work in L.A. or maybe a cushy houseband gig in Vegas. He practiced two to four hours a day to improve his chops, and he took singing lessons to make himself more marketable. At his peak, he was working with three bands at once: he'd do a buffet set at one hotel, a cocktail set at another, then end the night with six sets of dance trash with a five-piece at a top-forty lounge. But nothing good, nothing special, ever happened, and eventually he just wore himself down, settling finally for steady work six nights a week with a circuit regular called The Mystic Five.

Like every other band on the circuit, The Mystic Five was hoping to play some angle that would win them a better room. They had tried everything. At one point all of them dressed in drag to sing a Supremes medley, but that was being done already by another band, they learned later. Nothing was new, it seemed. Disillusioned, and weary from travel, the keyboardist quit to take a solo gig at a Reno steakhouse. Then the bass player packed up and went home to Sacramento. And the lead guitarist said he was going to open a music store with the money he'd saved over the years. And so it was over, and Erik was back at the Reno union asking the secretary to put his name on the players-available list, along with the rest of the loners and losers.

Just like that: one week he's got a steady gig, the next he's haunting the casinos handing out his card to other players, pimping himself for a paycheck.

He moved himself to a cheap motel on Fourth Street, started eating eggs and noodles in his room to save money, walked to the casinos to save gas, and wore his tuxedo every night to make a good impression. But the tux, frayed at the cuffs and shiny in the seat, needed replacing. He was beginning to feel like a bum, and it scared him. He worried that he reeked of desperation, so he rehearsed his pitch: "Hi, good set, guys, my name's. . . I've gigged with . . . I'm sure you've heard of . . . ." But nothing sounded natural, nothing sounded right. He'd always had a gig of some kind—there had always been a band in front of him. He wasn't used to being alone, not like this.

With the few connections he had, he managed to score some pick-up gigs, doing a wedding here and a convention there, but it was only enough to keep him from taking a "regular" job, not enough to keep him steady. He started gambling. He told himself he was doing it for fun, just something to divert his worry, but he got serious fast, because he was pretty good at blackjack. So good, in fact, he entertained the notion of doing it full time, driving from casino to casino and making just enough to keep himself fat. But his luck was only a streak, and when it ran out he was at Ruth's table. She was a strong dealer, which meant she didn't give up many hands. He thought she was heartless, the way she stared him down every deal—he could never tell what the hell she was thinking.

She spooked him.

That's what happened.

It was all he could do to keep from whimpering when he'd surrendered his last chips. And still Ruth looked on impassively, her well-powdered face above him like the wide, white glow of the moon. Her green eyes blinked once, her brows raised in question: Another hand?

He turned and stumbled from the table like a drunk. God, what had he come to?

Later, Ruth found him at the bar, downing drafts.

"Lordy, how you pity yourself," she said.

"You think so?" he said. She looked better here, in the dark, he thought. She was a small woman with bony arms and a tumble of too-red hair. Not his type. But she didn't look interested in him either. He read her name tag: Ruth.

"The way you look had me worried," she continued, staring at him as if trying to read an eye chart. "I figured to check on you."

He wanted to smirk at her, to show her that he was

as tough as she was, but he couldn't make his face work right. He thought of his motel room, of his drum kit stacked in one corner, each drum coffined in a black fiberboard case, his life amounting to nothing more than that, a room where he kept the TV on all the time just for the company. He felt his mouth quivering, then he heard himself say, "Take me home, Ruth."

She laughed. It wasn't a cruel laugh, just enough to tell him he didn't know what he was doing. Then she said, "You'll be all right."

He watched her walk away; she didn't look back.

The next night, he returned and sat at the bar nearest her table. He knew she saw him watching her because she wouldn't look him in the face. She was busy, the casino crowded, and he saw her beat player after player, until a bouncer—a kid with a thigh-thick neck and a flattop haircut—told him to leave if he wasn't going to play or drink. He said, "I'm waiting for Ruth."

The bouncer laid a big hand on his shoulder and said, "She ain't waiting for you, bud."

When Ruth left the casino after her shift, two hours later, Erik was waiting for her outside. She looked better than the night before—maybe he was getting used to her already, he thought, or maybe he was simply that desperate. He liked the way she walked, as if she were stepping through high grass, her eyes on the horizon.

He said, "You didn't have to bounce me, Ruth."

"I couldn't concentrate." She stopped to light a cigarette. A flock of tourists flowed around her on the sidewalk. She puffed once, twice, then exhaled, smoke drifting from her nostrils.

"You mean you like me," he said. He felt himself smiling.

She glanced at him, then continued walking. "You distract me," she said. "It ain't the same thing."

She took him home.

The next day he checked out of his motel for good.

He had every intention of making her happy. The

first week, he fixed her dinner, omelets and home fries, every day before she went to work. And he cleaned her condo, Windexing windows and Pinesoling sinks, even taking the time to dust her collection of horse figurines, which were lined along the windows and on the shelves everywhere. She'd been collecting the figurines, most of them made of glass, since she was a little girl, she said. And they were worth money, which surprised him because they looked like toys, girl toys.

She said she'd never had a man who cared for her things the way he seemed to care. "I do care," he told her. But he wondered if he cared only because he had nothing better to do right now. She was a comfort, it was true, but he'd been comfortable other times with other women.

She liked his hands; they were so sensitive, she said. And he was proud that she appreciated what he prized so highly.

"When I'm gigging," he explained, "I've got to be careful all the time: a careless flick of a kitchen knife, a clumsy reach for a doorknob, *anything*, could put me out of work."

She kissed his fingers, one by one. "You must've been scared," she said.

He realized that she was right. He had been scared.

After he lost the donut job, he started having nightmares about drumming. They weren't the usual dreams about forgetting the music or breaking the drums or walking onstage naked, they were about his hands: his hands would fall apart, like water-soaked tissue, clumps of flesh dropping from his fingers, his palms splitting.

He'd wake Ruth with his yelps of alarm and she'd try to comfort him, stroking his sweat-slick forehead. He'd grip her arm with both hands; he'd feel his pulse pushing at his fingertips. In the darkness, he'd picture her condo, the wall-to-wall peach carpet, the pink-flowered drapes, the horse figurines all around, the dim blue ghost of the Sierra Nevadas framed by her bedroom window. "I'm in Reno," he'd say, finally.

"With me," she'd add.

He'd let out a long breath. He'd say, "I got to start practicing again, Ruth."

"Then you practice," she'd say. "I want you happy."

But there wasn't any place to practice on a full kit. He'd have to rent a space where the noise wouldn't be a bother. That'd cost him plenty.

He said he wasn't going to borrow any more money from Ruth. So he took a temp job stacking empty boxes in a warehouse out by the interstate. Though it was easy work, he wore gloves to protect his hands. He wondered why anybody would want a warehouse full of empty cardboard boxes. The guy who stacked boxes with him worked there full-time. He was a big, messy man whose blue jeans always rode low on his wide hips, his shirttail bunched at the back, his jowly face poorly shaved, a ridge of whiskers showing just above the cheek or jaw on either side. He said, "You look like a wrangler with those gloves you're wearing, pal."

They were blue leather work gloves with wide denim collars at the wrists. Erik felt safe in them. "I'm a drummer," he said.

"That so?" The man stacked the empty boxes slowly. It was his life, after all. He said, "I build doghouses myself and sell them on the side."

"What?" It didn't make sense that someone would mention doghouses after drumming.

"Just got me a Craftsman table saw." The man smiled at the thought of it.

Hobbies. The man thought drumming was just a hobby, like building doghouses.

"You don't understand, I drum professionally. I'm in the musicians' union. I've played the Sands, the Hilton, Harolds—you name it."

It was important that Erik set this straight.

The man paused in his work and regarded him with mild surprise, as if to say, What the hell you talking about?

At lunch break, the warehouseman sent him to pick up sandwiches at the 7-Eleven. Once outside, the sun smart ing his eyes, the sky cloudless, Erik didn't want to go back to the warehouse. So he kept driving, past the 7-Eleven, past the truck depot, past the industrial park; he kept driving until he was downtown, in the logjam of tourist traffic. It was July, the streets clotted with flower-shirted colors, the casino signs competing in the glare of sunlight. The air was heavy with the smell of cigarette smoke, car exhaust, and baking asphalt.

He spent the afternoon roaming the casinos. He saw a few trios performing. None of the drummers was as good as he was, but he envied their gigs, envied that they were *making* something, that their music was *moving* the gamblers, who so often seemed unmovable—he saw toes tapping, heads nodding, old women mouthing words to love songs, old men whistling the melodies.

He bought a Reno Advertiser and scanned the "Musicians Wanted" columns. He saw an opening and he knew he could land it, he knew he was going back. The thought of it made his fingers grow cold with anticipation, his stomach fluttery. He wanted to play right now, to hit the heads, to feel the beat below him. What could be better than that?

The next morning, while he was eating a cold ham sandwich in front of the TV, Ruth said, "You quit your temp job, didn't you?"

"It was just empty boxes," he said.

She sat in the stuffed chair next to the TV. She had just gotten off work and was wearing her black-and-whites. "You've got to work somewhere," she said. She sounded sad.

He swallowed. "I'll get a gig."

She looked at him, "And go on the road?"

He saw her glance at the TV as if afraid of missing something there. A program about animals that did extraordinary tricks was on. She said, "I thought we'd started something."

"What's that supposed to mean?" He'd stopped chewing his sandwich, the bread like cotton in his mouth.

"*You and me*, didn't we start something?"

"Sure," he answered. "Sure we did."

But then she turned away again, back to the TV. He could see that her eyes were clouding, that she knew he was flaking on her like an alcoholic sideman, someone you need for the gig but know won't make it past the second set. He didn't like what he was doing, not one bit, but what choice did he have? Nothing made him feel as good as music.

Later, Ruth was especially loud in bed. It was as though she were in pain, trying to call him back. She shouted his name once or twice. It made him cringe inside; his heart felt as wasted as wilted lettuce. They had started something, hadn't they? As they lay side by side afterwards, staring up at the pale U cast by the street light outside the window, he said, "I love you, Ruth." It sounded like an apology.

He listened to her breathing.

"Liar," he heard her say at last.

She said it without malice, as if it was a reminder, a simple statement of fact. Then she got up to dress for work.

The last time he'd told a woman he loved her she had forced him to. She was a short-order cook at the El Dorado in Elko. *Tell me you love me*, she'd said, after they'd gone to his room. *Then we can fuck*. He did as she told him. Then she demanded more: *Tell me you love me more than you love your drums, tell me you'd stop tomorrow if I asked....* She pulled off her tank top, mussing her corkscrewed perm; her breasts above the snowy scallops of her bra were sunburned. *Tell me you'd do anything, almost anything, to taste what I've got for you...*

Ruth wasn't asking him to make choices like that. He could have drumming and her both, if that's what he wanted. But he knew she was right, he didn't love her. He liked going to her, liked being with her, but he didn't want to stay. She was too firmly fixed in place and he was still in motion—he didn't think he could stop, not now anyway, not yet. As a musician, he only had to be in one right place at one right moment to get the break he'd been waiting for all his professional life. Every player knew that much.

The next day, while Ruth slept, he auditioned for a cocktail trio and got the gig. He did well because he was fresh, eager to get back at it. The other players were younger than he by about ten years, but they had good chops. They said their gig in Fallon, a farming town two hours east, was just a warm-up for better gigs elsewhere, though they didn't say where the else was. Eventually they'd find their way back to Reno, they said. It was what Erik expected to hear.

He needed a new tuxedo, he needed gas money, he needed new sticks. Had he forgotten already how much it cost to keep this up?

"What's all this?" the pawnbroker asked him.

"They're figurines," Erik said. "Very valuable. They're old, I think."

The pawnbroker, a young man with a sallow face and one tooth missing up front, took a horse figurine from the box. "This one's a palomino," he said.

Did that make it worth more? Erik wondered. "They're collectibles," he said. "Everybody wants them."

The pawnbroker looked up at him and smirked. "Everybody but you, right?"

Like the thief he knew he was, Erik had sneaked the figurines out of Ruth's place while she was at work. He promised himself and—in a carefully-worded note—he promised Ruth that, in a month or so, he would bring back her collection. It was a loan, he told her. And it guaranteed their connection, didn't it? What he owed her. How much she had to trust him. When he returned from Fallon, maybe they could see if what they had started was something they wanted to continue.

The pawnbroker was peering into the two grocery boxes of horses. In one hand he scissored an unlit finger-sized cigar. His black T-shirt said, in pink letters, Play Tahoe!

"Most are glass," said Erik.

"I see that," the pawnbroker said, still looking.

"I'm going to buy them back soon, don't forget."

The pawnbroker nodded. "Right. Your ticket's good for sixty days."

He gave Erik just enough to buy a used tux at the Groom's Palace, with a little left over for travel expense.

There was time to kill before Erik left town the next morning. He couldn't stay at the condo—the place felt too small for him now—and he didn't want to waste money on a motel, so he packed his station wagon, parked in a security lot, then roamed the casinos, where he could waste the night. He was wearing his new used-tux because it made him feel better—it marked him as Entertainment, setting him apart from gambling bums and tourists.

The casinos were crowded and noisy, bells ringing, barkers calling in passersby. In the casinos there were no clocks, no shadows, no reminders of anything lapsed. And everybody, it seemed, had the flu of hope. Everywhere Erik looked he saw eager fingers clawing coins from the catch-alls of the slots, croups pushing chip stacks across the green felt of the tables, the winners yelping in disbelief, "I won! I won!," as if they'd just been mortally wounded.

But Erik had been in Nevada long enough to know that you had to drop a lot before you got a return, if you got one at all. The odds were always in favor of the house. So he sat at the nickel slots, where he couldn't do much damage.

He kept picturing himself on the road, the flat expanse of desert before him, the treeless Nevada mountains like dark ships on the horizon, and the sky as empty as he felt right now.

He lost twenty bucks in half as many minutes. He was feeding in five coins at a time and yanking the slot arm so hard the machine shuddered from the force of it. He was angry. With so much luck so near, why wasn't he a winner? He wasn't that old, after all. Plenty of musicians older than he had done better. And he wasn't asking for that much.

As he yanked the slot arm again, he realized he'd have done almost anything to continue gigging, anything for one more pull of the handle.

He imagined Ruth alone in her condo, the window ledges and shelves empty of her horses. She'd catalog them in her mind, trying to remember each one, where it used to stand and how she had come by it. But she wouldn't be able to account for them all, there were so many, and, later, she'd find herself remembering forgotten ones and forgetting remembered ones—it'd keep her up nights, all those horses.

An hour later, he was grateful to find the pawnshop open. Then he remembered: hell, the pawnshops are always open in Reno. The broker eyed him with mild surprise, a hint of a smirk on his face. Must feel good to be on that side of the counter, standing a couple feet above the customers, asshole.

"You got more glass horses?" the broker asked. Making a joke.

Erik pictured Ruth's as shooting targets shattered across the backyard. That's how his life felt. He hefted his black canvas tote—as big around as a cocktail table—onto to counter. "Cymbals," he announced. "I want the horses back."

"What kind of cymbals?"

He had never pawned a piece of his set. Never. It seemed the beginning of the end for him. Next thing, maybe he'd think he didn't need his floor tom. Where would it stop?

"I'll trade you an Avedis Zyldian ride, eighteen inches, first series, from the fifties, hand hammered brass—probably worth five hundred easy, so you'll have to give me the difference." Erik paused for a breath. He still hadn't convinced himself that he'd be comfortable using his sixteen-inch crash cymbal as a ride, but it would have to do.

The broker was lighting up one of those finger-thin cigars with a vintage silver Zippo. He inhaled a mouthful of odorous smoke, squinted down at Erik, then said evenly, "I'll give you the horses and fifty bucks."

"Very funny."

The broker shrugged, his eyes to the ceiling. "That's my offer."

Like dealing with an agent. It seemed there would

always be someone like this in his life, making demands he could hardly abide. Ruth had the pit bosses to deal with. Bartenders had the food and beverage managers eyeing them constantly. As good as he might make himself, as hard as he might work, there would always somebody looking down, always somebody with an advantage over him.

He thought of Ruth lying on the couch, her feet in his lap, the blue-red glow of the TV the only light on in the room. He heard her telling him he was a good man—what she said every time he massaged her feet: *You're a good man, Erik, that feels right, a really good man, a little lower, thanks, a man with talented hands.*

He looked down now at his talented hands. They were digging into his pockets as if searching for a good excuse, something that would help Ruth understand how it was a good man like him could leave her this way, without a decent goodbye or a thank-you or a single glass horse to her name.

He had nearly put all of the horses back by the time she returned home—early—carrying a bag of groceries. Dawn was a pink-orange glow beyond the bumpy silhouette of the eastern range, which Erik could see through the open door. It would be a hot, hot day, he could tell, already the window AC units working hard, the air damp with morning heat.

"What're you doing?" she asked, eyeing his tuxedo up and down. She looked startled, a little scared, maybe angry too, as if she'd caught him with another woman.

"Cleaning," he said. He knew this made no sense, but he saw no advantage in telling her the truth. It was enough that she had her collection back. Nothing else had changed. He was still leaving. She would still be angry.

"You got a gig?" she said. She closed the door behind her with a push of her black running shoe, stepped over to the kitchen counter, then set down the groceries. He saw a steak on top big enough for two.

"In Fallon," he said hopefully, wanting her to want

his success at least half as much as he wanted it.

She nodded at the name, as if considering the possibilities. She looked tired, older than he wanted her to look.

"They don't have shit there for casinos," she said. "You'll be bored."

He shrugged. "It's a gig. The players are pretty good."

"Two hours east," she said. She began putting away the groceries, the fridge door open. "Maybe you can visit me."

"That'd be okay with you?"

Now she shrugged as if to say, Sure, why not?

"What time you leave?" she asked. She looked up, a Styrofoam carton of extra-large eggs in one hand. No cloudy eyes this time. No regrets. Her strength made him want to stay. Where would he find another Ruth?

"Soon," he said. He set the last horse on the shelf. The palomino, a figure nearly as big as his hand. It was posed in mid-run. He thought of mustangs in the desert—they were numerous, supposedly, but for as long as he'd been driving Nevada, from the California side to Utah, countless days and nights, he'd never seen them.

"I'll make you breakfast if you want," Ruth said.

Embarrassed by her graciousness, Erik muttered, "Thanks," then sat at the kitchen counter, grateful for the time remaining, for the competent noise of Ruth's cooking, for the chance to see once more the skill of her sure hands, the knowing way she cracked eggs without ruining the yolk—a reminder of the way she dealt cards without losing nerve and, he realized, the way she handled his heart.

the Ape in Me

I'm supposed to strangle this beautiful young woman today but my heart's not in it. Toni, my girlfriend, tells me I should be used to it by now, I've murdered so many women. But that's the problem: I'm tired of being the heavy. Just once I'd like to be somebody's sidekick or the nice guy whose untimely death makes the audience sob with regret. Listen, I'm realistic. I'm not asking for a big piece, just a different angle, a character I can like for once. Because, honest to God, I'm starting to get nightmares about these things, finding myself really killing people on the set but not meaning to—losing my touch. When I wake up, I can still see the crew's terrified faces, their fingers aimed at me: "Christopher, what have you done?" I hear them crying.

Back in the fifties, when I started out, it was much easier. I was an ape then. There were only two or three top apes in town at the time and, though they had studied apes plenty in an amateur way, I was something of an expert, having taken two years of primate biology at UCLA. I was planning on being a researcher, maybe going on for my Ph.D., but I got sidetracked after answering a call for "apemen" put out by a low-budget studio. They made a very forgettable picture about radiation turning some Pacific Island ers into gorillas, and I got to parade around as their king. I was that good. Though the suit was poorly ventilated and very heavy (seventy-five pounds), the playacting was a lot of fun—I could hardly believe I was getting paid for it. After the shoot, the director asked me if I'd like to do another gorilla part. To continue working, I had to join the union. I did the second picture, then I started getting enough calls to make me think I didn't need school, the money was so good.

"What am I supposed to tell my customers?" my father asked me. He was a barber downtown. "My son quit UCLA to become a Hollywood ape?" My mother told him not to worry, it was only a phase. "Sure," he said, "my son's ape phase." He pointed his scissors at me. "You'll regret this, Christopher. How long you think you can wear that costume before you lose your mind?"

It was years before my parents would accept any money from me. "Hollywood jungle money," my father called it. But after he went bankrupt, in 1965, he didn't complain anymore, though it truly saddened me to imagine his grimace every time he deposited the check I'd sent. Mailing him the money allowed both of us to pretend it didn't matter.

Since I'm an L.A. kid born and bred, I didn't think Hollywood could make me dizzy with ambition. But it did. I wanted to be the best ape ever. The advantage I had over the other apes was my youth. I was only twenty-one, and I had a good build because I'd been a shot putter on the UCLA track team. To do the ape right, you have to have some weight and girth. I made a point of working out long before working out became fashionable, and it paid off until I started getting injured.

Had I been allowed to be an ape and only an ape, one that pounds its chest to startle a safari, say, or one that lurches around in a cage at a circus, I might not have hurt myself. But, in Hollywood, an ape's never just an ape—he's always running amok, strangling somebody or slinging a screaming girl over his shoulder or clambering across a steep rooftop before jumping the hero. The Hollywood ape is always fighting and always getting killed—falling from a tree, a rooftop, a mountain.

So very quickly I learned how to be a stunt man, doing whatever the director told me to do, because I really didn't know any better. It didn't occur to me that I had any choice in the matter. After all, I prided myself on being what they called a "reasonable" actor, which meant that I never said no. Sometimes I got hurt so badly I'd lay immobilized all weekend, popping aspirin every hour, just so I could make the call on Monday. I managed to stay away from the pills that started showing up on the set in the sixties; I thought liquor was just as good an anesthetic. Drinking cost me two marriages and some good work, and I can only remember half of what I did from '67 to '72.

My "big break" came in 1964 when I played a zombie strangler. It was my first role out of costume (by this time I'd had three gorilla suits custom-made): the camera showed my face, and from then on playing apes was only a sideline. I became a "killer" of every kind: werewolf, vampire, space invader, mutant, zombie, ghoul, ghost, body snatcher, psychopath.... Now, instead of the weighty costume, I was wearing all sorts of rubber pieces and patches on my face. Prosthetics, they call it nowadays. Back then we just called it glove rubber. It ruined my skin, the latex heated up so badly. I've got pores the size of pencil pricks in a peach, which would have spoiled me for closeups had I been anything but a monster. It affected my eyes too. Gave me recurring bacterial buildup on my lids—called blepharitis—which makes me bloodshot half the time.

"You shouldn't ever give up hope," Toni tells me. "You could become another Nightmare Eddie."

She means the guy who's made nine slasher pictures that have a big cult following. Nightmare Eddie even has a doll out now that his kiddy fans carry around: it spits "blood."

I say, "Toni, I couldn't sleep at night knowing I'm that kind of memory for children."

"You take this stuff too seriously," she says. "You know it's all a game. Cash in while you can!"

Toni's young enough to be the daughter I never had. I met her last year when one of the security guards was trying to throw her off the set of a picture I was working. "She's with me," I told the guy. She was snapping photos of the actors' hands and feet. That's her thing. She's got her first show coming out in a little West Hollywood gallery soon. Nothing but hands and feet of actors, some real famous, some not famous at all, like me. I've got wide stubby-fingered hands which she finds especially sexy, she says.

I let Toni move in the first week we were together. At my age, I try not to be overcautious because I've already made so many mistakes one more won't matter. Compared to my two ex-wives, Toni's a welcome change, because she's got no plans for me. We're just "cruising," as she puts it. She's a tall, bony girl with a helmet haircut and a pale complexion. She dresses like most young women nowadays, wearing men's clothes half the time, baggy shirts and work boots, and either too much makeup or none at all.

She says she likes me for my experience, which is a nice way of saying I don't slobber all over her like the twenty-year-olds she's used to "seeing." And she truly worries that I worry too much about my career. I've got another good ten years or so left on the set and I'd like to make them count. Toni says whatever I do will count because I'm good. "It's not the part," she says, a true coach at heart, "it's how you play it, right? Nobody kills as good as you do, Chris. Give yourself some credit."

But killing's not what it used to be, I tell her. Together we watch Super 8s from my private collection and I show her how it was done "in the old days." *Tasteful,* I tell her. "It was more effect than special effect, if you know what I mean."

"You mean no blood and guts," she says.

Nowadays a big-screen killing's rarely clean, because the special effects crews have taken over. They're just kids, most of them, and they make themselves giddy with the mechanicals, trying to outdo whatever trick they most admired in a competitor's sequence. In the picture I'm doing now, I'm supposed to strangle the girl so badly her head falls off. It sounds stupid, I know, but that's the state of the "art" nowadays.

Toni always goes with me for moral support, which I've really needed lately. I don't know what would've happened to me this last year if she hadn't been around, because work's been pretty tough. I haven't been sleeping as well as I'd like. All those bad dreams.

The truth is, Toni could do better than me, though maybe I should give her more credit for knowing what she's into. After all, she's already used to rubbing me down when my back's in spasms and icing my ankles after a hard day.

A couple months ago I took her out to the field to show her how I used to throw shot. I guess, like any infatuated fifty-five-year-old, I felt I had something to prove. I told Toni I was going to start working with my shot again to help keep down my paunch. I don't think she cared one way or the other. "You're a big guy," she said, "you should have some paunch." As I circled for my put, I pictured that iron ball sailing fifty feet in a lovely arc over the field. I got only one chance to try, however, because the throw pulled a muscle below my right clavicle, which took two weeks to heal. I was in such pain I couldn't even raise my arm, and Toni had to carry the shot back—it hadn't traveled more than ten feet.

For the picture I'm doing now my face is pretty clean. All they've stuck me with is some purple lumps on my head, which I had to shave for the part. Makeup's made me greenish-white, my eyes awfully deep-set. I'm supposed to be a man who's gone mad from eating too much junk food. A "cereal killer," the crew jokes. I'm just one of several berserks in the picture, but my sequence is the longest and most complicated. I am the old pro, after all.

I've already done the junk food takes, so now it's the finale, after which I'll be killed off, as usual. I can't tell you how many times I've been killed. That's the only thing

I envy of Nightmare Eddie's pictures—he never dies. Dying used to be hard for me because it made me think of my parents and how close they are to their end. And getting closer every day. I know, we're all supposed to be grown-up about death, accept the inevitable and all that. But I worry. And now, for the first time in my life, I've started worrying about my own end. I might have welcomed death years ago, when I was living low, but now things are just starting to get good for me. With Toni, I think I've finally got a stab at happiness.

"Trained" actors, I've heard, can "distance" themselves from the emotional weight of a death scene, but I've never learned this trick. It'd be easier for me if I didn't always play such horrible characters. I mean, I've committed so many truly terrible acts, maiming and mutilating so many people, that when it comes time to die all I want is a chance to make restitution. *Hey, I can make good!* I want to tell the hero as he corners me. *Give me another chance!*

I phoned my agent recently and told him I'd like to try something different. I said, "Give me something lighter, Hal. I could be somebody's kindly, retarded uncle."

"What're you saying, Chris?" I pictured him at his table with glossy 5 X 10s scattered before him like trading cards. "You're getting bigger roles than you ever have."

"Bloodier roles, Hal, uglier roles. This is not what I got into pictures for, is it?"

"You're asking me?" he said. "You've got a good rep, Chris, my friend. You kill good, you die good. You do stunts. Why do you want more?"

"I want something likeable, Hal."

"Oh, *please*, Chris, what is this, Mr. Sensitive week?"

"Hal, I'm serious."

"*I* like you, Chris. The studios like you. I don't understand. Are you going through some male menopausal thing or what?"

"Can you help me or not, Hal?"

I didn't want to threaten him, but I think he got the message: either he'd help me or I'd get another agent. So he said he'd see what he could do. That was three months ago. So far he hasn't offered me anything except an audition for the Chichimanga Chicken spot in a local ad campaign.

"Don't scoff," he told me. "This is a talking part, it shows your face, *and* if this chain does well, it could go national."

He was right, it wasn't so bad. But I just couldn't put myself in another animal suit.

The Director of my current shoot is a kid who's no more than thirty, but already he's made big bucks and a name for himself as a horror king. The Prince of Darkness, the trades call him. As I walk onto the set he says, "Christopher, your last takes were fly, pal, in the pocket. You up for the big one?"

"Lead the way," I tell him. I glance around for Toni, who's standing next to the best boy. She nods encouragement, as if to say, this'll be a good one, I just know it. She's dressed like an extra, wearing a polka-dotted jumper and yellow rubber Wellingtons, her hair knotted in a single sprout at the top of her head.

I think I love her.

The actress I'm supposed to kill is a pretty blonde named Carla who can't be more than seventeen. She looks like she's done some modeling before getting this break. She's so eager for approval, she hardly listens to what the Director's saying.

She's staring at me like I scare her.

She says, "You'll be careful with those big hands of yours, won't you, Chris?"

I smile politely. "They haven't failed me yet, Carla." If only she knew how little I trust them today, how many times they've betrayed me in my dreams.

As the soundman angles the boom and the cameras roll up, I notice that I'm surrounded by youngsters: except for one cameraman, everybody here looks under forty. Where have all the oldsters gone?

The Director calls "action" and I stumble into the

frame, doing a kind of zombie walk that I've nearly made famous, my spastic arms clawing the air. I work fast, and the camera crew is good, so it doesn't take us long to get the several shots we need to introduce me in the sequence.

Then it's time for the kill.

As usual, the victim stumbles, this time over a kitchen chair, and I catch her while she's down. Then we cut to some head shots to show my menace and her horror. And finally I get to put my paws around Carla's lovely neck. It makes me a little giddy to hold her that way, because for the moment she's all mine, no more than a mannequin, really. To keep herself steady, she holds onto my shirt front while I pretend to squeeze the life out of her. She's gasping. I'm gurgling with perverse delight. I can feel the pulse of her jugular against the fingers of my right hand. The nape of her neck is sweaty. A bit of saliva rolls from her mouth—she's better than I thought she'd be—and her eyes roll to show whites only.

I've done this so many times it feels very natural, very real. The girl garbles a final gasp, then her head rolls back and her arms drop, the weight of her now freely in my hands. It gives me a shiver to watch her die like that, and for a terrible moment I think maybe I've really killed her, she's now so limp. Suddenly I want to release her to see if she's okay, but I can't break the scene because I know it's a real good one. It may be my best strangle yet. CPR, I'm thinking, could rouse her. It's not too late. I shake her one last time, roughly, in hopes that her eyelids will flutter.

Then the Director shouts, "Cut!" And the girl is abruptly disengaging herself from my grip. "Thanks," she says. She steps back to let the dresser fix her hair.

The Director says, "Chris, I liked how you shook her once at the end. We'll see if we can keep that."

I'm pleased to hear a compliment, and I turn to share my smile with Toni, who fingers a V for victory. Then I see her snap a shot of a boom-girl's hand.

It wasn't so bad, I'm thinking. Really, it wasn't so bad. And I did good, didn't I? The Director makes us do two more takes for insurance. Then Carla disappears and the effects crew comes in with a doll that looks just like her. It's made of wax, rubber, and God knows what else. Her face shows a wide-eyed, open-mouthed gag of horror. I point out to the Director that when I strangled the girl her eyes were not staring at me like this. He tells me not to worry, the continuity people will handle it. One of the effects kids, a boy who's trying to grow a goatee, explains to me how to mangle the doll so the head wrenches off and the blood starts spurting.

When I begin to strangle the thing, I tell myself it's just a piece of wax and plastic, even though the effects kids are pumping air into it to make the thing jerk and flinch like a real person. It gives me the creeps, and I'm hoping the disgust I feel doesn't show in the shot. I'm wrenching the neck and wrenching it, gasping with effort—I imagine the screams the sound people will dub in later—then suddenly the head tears away from the neck, the girl's eyes bulging, blood seeping from the ears: purple and scarlet veins are spewing blood. And the <u>bone</u>, I didn't imagine there'd be bone, but now I see the spinal column attached to the dangling head, the blood pouring, pouring forth, a ridiculously hideous show that nearly makes me retch. Behind me I hear somebody gasp. The Director says, calmly, "Cut. Good take. Let's see what we've got."

While he watches the playback, I stand there with the doll, which is still leaking syrupy blood at my feet. "Don't move, Chris," the Director tells me. Already the syrup is drying on my hands, a sticky scarlet goop that makes me wonder, Is real blood like this? The effects kids probably know. They've probably experimented.

When I look to the shadows off-camera I expect to see Toni nodding to me, as if to say, "You're doing good, Chris." But she's talking to one of the crew.

"Okay," the Director says, clapping his hands. "Let's do it again."

The effects kids bring out *another* dummy identical to the other.

"The take no good?" I ask.

The Director pauses to lift and resettle his Angels
cap on his head. He says, "There wasn't enough *emotion*,
Christopher. I need more from you."

"Emotion?" I ask.

Assistants are cleaning me up, wiping my hands.
Somebody's dabbing my face with makeup.

"No, *passion*—I guess that's the word." The Director glances down at the floor, where the cleanups are mop-
ping away the blood syrup. Wearing jeans and a "DO IT!" T-
shirt, he's a tall, gawky guy, the kind of kid I might've picked
on in high school. "Yeah," he says, looking at me again, "I
think passion is the thing." He narrows his eyes. "Strangle
her, Chris, like you *love* her."

I'm nodding "yes, yes, of course," like I understand,
but it's just reflex. I don't really understand. I can't tell you
how many times I've been in this situation, where I have
no idea what the director's asking for. As usual, I'll improvise, doing whatever seems right as the scene unfolds, then
I'll pretend that this is exactly what the director has called
for. Most of them, especially the younger ones, don't know
the difference.

We set up the shot again, the doll in my grasp, her
startled face glaring up at me. I think of the real girl, Carla,
who modeled this expression, of all the hope she has for
her life: only seventeen and all those roles waiting, all those
possibilities beckoning.

Twenty, ten, even two years ago I would've told her
it isn't her we want, it's only her graceful neck, say, or her
eyes, which are suitable for closeups, or the way her mouth
looks when she screams, but it isn't *her*, so she should stop
dreaming of a great future as an actress, stop thinking of
herself as special. When I was at my lowest, it didn't seem
I was anything more than a convenience on the set: big
enough to play the part and not so handsome that I couldn't
be made to look hideous.

When Toni came along, though, it was difficult to
be that cynical, because she's hardly twenty-one and already

her career's taken off. Would I tell *her* she didn't stand a chance?

"You got more hope than you let on," she said. She was right. So here's something I've never admitted: I'd like to play one part my parents might enjoy. One picture they could walk away from smiling.

"Ready, Christopher?" I hear the Director call.

I take a deep breath. My concentration's shattered. "Roll it."

I hear the scene-board clap. And we're on. *We?* Just me and the dummy of the girl. "A nice girl," I hear my mother saying. "Why would anyone want to harm a nice girl like that?" "And nice hair too," my father says. "She takes good care. Look how shiny. You got to like somebody with good grooming."

What will Carla's father think when he sees her strangled on the big screen? Will he say with pride, "That's my girl!" Or will he shudder, the movie his own private nightmare, his palms sweaty, his heart bleating from the pit of his stomach: "Stop it! Stop it! My Baby!"

The girl/dummy's eyes bulge as I wrench her neck.

I have a fear that I'll wake up one night to discover I've strangled Toni. "Talk about bringing your work home with you!" Toni jokes.

I hear my father's words, see him shaking his scissors at me, twenty-some years ago: "How long you think you can wear that costume before you lose your mind?"

Carla's father will see his girl decapitated on the big screen. Why shouldn't that make him crazy too?

But what if, at the critical moment, just as it seems that I have all but strangled the life from her slender body, just as I am about to rip off her lovely head, what if I relented?

What if at this moment I touched the girl's cheek with one finger to wipe away the tears—*my* tears, the monster weeping over her in remorse—and uttered the first words I've uttered in years?

I feel my mouth working up the words as if they

were gobs of fat stuck in my throat. I'm choking with a need to speak.

I hear a growl. Is that what comes out finally?

"A monster is like a cat," Toni told me recently. "He kills anything he comes upon, anything that moves, anything small that catches his attention. He can't help himself—it's just the way he is. So don't fight it, Chris, just be who you are."

I'm sorry. That's what I wanted to say. *I'm sorry.* But it doesn't come. And already the girl's dying, her last terror-filled glare a kind of vengeful promise of the hauntings her killer will endure.

A monster never relents, it seems.

Now, the job finished, the girl draped over my arm like a wet overcoat, I sense the excitement on the set, the spectators all but breathless—tempted to applaud as soon as the Director gives the word. And I wait for it, breathless myself. This may be my best strangle yet.

High Heat for Cotton

T his is what she knew: He worked at Britches, where he got a twenty-percent discount on clothes but not on shoes. He was a buttoned-down oxford and khaki kind of guy, always in loafers, never in wingtips, and never sockless. No argyles, either. White or navy crews mostly. She had watched him every evening, five to nine, from her station at Casual Corner, where she got a ten-percent discount. If she were assistant manager, as she hoped to be, she would never have had the time for peering over the sales rack—spying—when she should've been marking inventory. But, as it was, things were slow. The recession and all.

Unlike her, he was part-time. She could tell. He arrived every other day at 4:30 or 4:45. He was young, probably a college man, since he was dressed as she imagined college men should, though she wasn't sure what college he belonged to. Could've been Loyola or Goucher, definitely not Towson, but maybe Hopkins, though he didn't strike her as big-headed at all. She imagined he drove a Mazda two-door, something fast but nothing red and no custom plates. He wasn't pushy, that was the thing. He just stood there, hands clasped behind his back, his chin up, smiling easily at the customers but not diving for them like

the others did. Sharks at feeding time, everyone on commission.

She'd been watching for two weeks, letting him
settle into the rhythm of the mall. Maybe he didn't know
this: every mall has its own rhythm. She had worked in
three sor far, and this one was the best yet. It rivaled Owings
Mills and drew a similar clientele, the prep school, pony-
owning suburbanites. Sometimes she lied to them, telling
them she liked what they liked and wore what they wore,
though really she had no money and her wardrobe was
shamefully limited. She was working on it, of course, but it
was only her creativity, her ability to mix and match, to
disguise herself in so many simple ways, that enabled her
to look as good as she did.

Like him, she was natural fibers all the way. Wools,
silks, and cottons. Her secret, her small but embarrassing
secret, was that she perspired too much—she'd ruin silk in
an hour! —and so she had to wear garment protectors, sti-
fling powder puff-sized pads strapped under her arms. She
imagined that if she made love to a man, she'd have to sneak
these off somehow; it was one of those little annoyances,
those small imperfections, that might ruin a magic moment.
So she worried.

Tonight she was wearing her only silk: a puff-sleeved,
ivory-colored blouse with shoulder pads. She always wore
shoulder pads because she needed the balance. Her waist
was small and her shoulders narrow, and a little slumped,
but her hips were fairly wide. Good for babies, a doctor
had once told her. But not too wide. Not so wide that, like
the assistant manager, she'd starve herself on Quick Slim
protein shakes.

To complement the blouse, she wore a pleated knee-
length wool skirt, white snowflake textured stockings, and
dun-colored flats. Heels were out of the question. Her
mother had lived a life in heels and her feet were now nearly
crippled—bunioned, callused, and gnarled. Like witch's feet.

"You gonna talk to him or what?" her friend, and
fellow sales associate, asked. Her friend was twenty and

pregnant already. She hadn't decided whether or not to keep the baby. The father was either someone she knew at American U., a junior, or her sociology instructor, a T.A. at Towson.

"I'm going to take a break when he does."

Her friend nodded her head as if to confirm a profound understanding. "If you two aren't meant for each other, I don't know who is."

She had told herself this very thing—and even though she didn't know his name yet (she wished Britches employees wore tags), she imagined he would feel the same way as soon as he saw her. Maybe he had already noticed her—it was hard to tell. His store was directly across from hers. And they both worked near the entrance. See? Already their lives were parallel.

If he asked, she'd tell him the truth, that she wasn't in college. This much she had decided. You couldn't start something like this with lies. But she was *saving* for college, wasn't she? And she did have the assistant manager's position coming her way. So it wasn't like she was a loser. Still, she worried about competing with the coeds, those perky girls from the Northeast, with their wardrobes and their money. But they weren't the real world. He'd see that much.

The mall was crowded, but not as crowded as it should've been, since it was a week before Christmas. She had learned that if the mall was a good one, the seasonal touches would make a difference, as they did here: garlands of real pine boughs; spruce trees decorated in single motifs (one in silver tinsel, another with bright red artificial apples, and yet another with handmade angels); a brass band that played Christmas carols three nights a week, a twenty-five member choir to sing those same carols the other three nights, and then, on Sunday afternoon, a soprano from the city opera and her pianist: she sang such soaring notes that it seemed the domed and finely latticed skylight would shatter like shards of ice over the listeners' heads. There were life-sized toy reindeer, too, and a Santa who looked truly

Santa-like, old and heavy, wearing a costly red velvet suit and well-polished leather boots that creaked as he stepped up to his throne.

Only if pressed would she now admit that recently, fewer than six months ago, she had been working at Lanlee Dress Outlet in the Dundalk Mall, an embarrassing sprawl of cut-rate shops under one low roof on the city's south-east side. Dundalk had a single fountain as its centerpiece and no amount of decoration would have made the place less depressing. But that's how it was southside. No money. Few prospects.

"He's *going*," she heard her friend say behind her.

He was leaning over the counter at the register, his trim backside turned to the doorway. Well-creased char-coal slacks tonight with tasseled cordovan loafers, a pink oxford, and a navy V neck. His hair, she noticed, was cleanly squared above the neck. No ducktails. And no wet look. His neck was thin, almost girlish. An intellectual's neck, maybe. And there was no epaulet-rise of muscled shoulder as he straightened up. She imagined he read novels and had hobbies.

He would appreciate her inclination to write him. She had started several letters. Each had a different ap-proach. Aggressive: "You don't know me, but maybe you should...." Sentimental: "You don't know me, but I feel that I know you already...." Demure: "You don't know me, but I was wondering if perhaps...." Philosophical: "You don't know me, but do any of us really know one another?"

None of them was right.

She had always written letters to people she ad-mired, people she hated, people she loved. Letters she never sent. She saved them in binders that, later, she taped shut for privacy. Here's the terrible lesson she learned about saving secrets: last year when she came home from the mall—a dull, too-long day at Dundalk—she found her mother at the kitchen table reading the notebooks, which she had kept shelved among her old albums and scrapbooks in her room. "Those are *mine*!" she had yelped. Panicked, she gathered the notebooks into her arms as if to save them from fire. That's what she'd felt like, her house was on fire. Her mother smiled at her with that broken what's-the-matter? look. It made her feel like the little girl she knew her mother would forever believe her to be. "These are precious," her mother said finally. "Did you write them in high school?" But, actually, she was asking something else: Did you really send these? "What difference does it make?" she said. She saw her mother blink in confusion.

It was then, or shortly after, that she decided to move out of her mother's house on Fort Avenue and away from South Baltimore forever. Away from the crowds of gray Formstone townhouses, the narrow treeless streets, the stink of inner harbor mud. "But you've got your own room here," her mother told her, following her around the house as she gathered her things. "You grew up here." As if this would make her reconsider. She paused to reply, her underclothes bunched in her hands. But there was nothing to say. She could only stare at her mother's newly permed hair, which reeked of salon treatment, the brown eyes flecked with green, the once-beautiful face—her own face—heavily made up to disguise the wear of years. She pitied the woman. Her mother had no idea who she was.

Seven years before, her father had left in a similar way. Back then it had been the two of them, mother and daughter, following Dad through the house as he gathered his things. But she couldn't recall what was said, only that she had blamed her mother for somehow chasing him away. She knew now that things are never so simple, never so one-sided. She had already been through one serious relationship—more serious than anything she had dreamed of in high school. The man was the manager of a Revco at Crosshaven, the first mall she had worked at, and she had learned then, after a painful five-month romance, that there are many good reasons for leaving.

Now she heard the part-timer, the college boy— her young man—laughing with another young man at the register. A sense of humor—would she be able to get what was funny? She took things too seriously, she feared. She wasn't *ironic* enough, maybe because she still couldn't quite fathom what it was, irony. "Take everything to mean the opposite of what it says," her friend explained. So when somebody means *love,* you think *hate*? She imagined that the well-dressed girls at Loyola or Goucher or Hopkins were ironic, smirking at everything someone like her might say. How could she compete?

"Well, here's the trick," her friend advised, "you *don't.*"

But the friend herself couldn't explain how to do this. Everybody was competing, after all: the sales associates on the floor of every shop competed against each other for the best commission, the stores in the mall competed against each other, the mall itself competed against other malls in town.

There wasn't a day she didn't think about competition, especially when she passed the hard-bodied mannequins in the shop windows, their hands held just so, their legs spread too far apart, their faces upturned, as if the passers-by weren't worth watching.

There he goes, her young man!

She felt heat rush to the tips of her ears as she stepped into the concourse crowd. She followed him. He walked with easy strides and free-swinging arms as if he never worried what others might think. Now so close, she saw that he wasn't as tall as she had thought. More like five-ten than six-two. He was headed for Cuisine Court, she was sure. She pictured herself sitting with him at Les Baguettes, where they could pretend they were *al fresco* in Paris, the skylight above them like the yellow glow of a late-afternoon sky. A French sky.

In her imagination she had watched the two of them together, just as she had once watched Snow White and the Seven Dwarfs in her 3-D View-Master as a girl, each colorful picture frozen for her scrutiny. There was no beginning, no end, only the circles of snapshots that showed his hand in hers, the two of them laughing at something, the two of them walking somewhere, the two of them waving at some-body.

While draping new green and red streamers from the light fixtures, her friend had said, "If I were you, I'd get my wheels washed." In case he walked her to her car. She promised herself she wouldn't be embarrassed by the rusted '93 Civic she was driving. But appearances did matter. That's why she wouldn't invite him to her apartment, if it came to that. Hers was a sparsely furnished efficiency, whose small windows looked onto the beltway. Some nights the traffic sounded to her like the wash of waves on a distant beach.

He stopped at Cinnabon to buy a roll, the air sud-denly warm and cinnamony, the pastries steaming in their trays. Down the corridor, the carolers were singing "God Rest Ye Merry Gentlemen," their voices echoing in the great dome above. The music sounded sad to her, like a kind of longing.

Let nothing you dismay….

She realized she hadn't decided how the meeting would begin. She was standing behind the young man. Waiting, ready to tap his shoulder?

Walk away?

Weep?

When she turned to sit at a nearby table, she, nearly breathless, sat abruptly with him. As if she had just col-lapsed, unable to go any further, having shopped all after-noon. And this was the only seat available. His blue-gray eyes blinked once. Her heart was pulsing loudly in her head—she heard Big Ben chimes—she said, "I'm your neigh-bor from across the way, at Casual."

She extended her hand.

In one hand he held a fist-sized cinnamon bun on a small sheaf of tissue paper, in the other a Styrofoam cup of black coffee. He said, "Hi." Then he smiled almost and nod-ded politely. He needed a shave, she noticed, but his face was well-kept and unblemished—only he looked older than she had thought he would.

She told him her name.

He told her his.

She said, "I hear you get a good discount at Britches."

"Pretty good," he said, nodding. "Now if only I could afford the clothes." He bit into the cinnamon bun. A smear of white icing clung to his upper lip.

"You've done a lot of retail?"

He looked up from his bun as if surprised that she was still sitting there. "I've worked Radio Shack, Kenny's Shoes, Kay Bee Toys, General Nutrition, Eddie Bauer—you want me to keep going?" He took another too-big bite.

This wasn't the way she had imagined it would be. But, then, she couldn't remember exactly what she had imagined. She said, "Malls mostly?"

She wanted to wipe clean his upper lip.

"Is there anyplace else to work?" he said. He spoke with his mouth full, then took a sip of coffee.

"I thought you were in college," she said. Too quickly, she realized.

He paused in mid-chew. "Who told you that?"

She shrugged. Was he irritated?

"*You* in college?" he asked. Still chewing.

"I'm saving for it," she said.

"Good for you."

Was this ironic?

He took a tentative sip of his coffee.

"What're you going to study?" he said.

She noticed that she had been stripping a Cinnabon napkin into shreds; the table was messy with it now. She stopped doing it. She heard the carolers singing "Silent Night," a child crying behind her, then someone nearby saying, "How do I know where it is? *You* tell me."

She shrugged finally. "I haven't decided yet."

He nodded, as if this was what he expected to hear.

"You're not studying anything?" she asked.

He was still chewing. "I'm studying for a full-time position."

Was that a joke? She waited for more. She was staring at his well-starched shirt cuffs, which had inched out from under his sweater. She was thinking—*high heat for cotton.* Did he iron his own shirts? A terrible chore.

He said, "I was studying computer at Essex."

Community College.

"But I got bored," he said.

As he spoke, she saw the wet dough roll over her young man's tongue like a lump of gray laundry through the porthole of a dryer. The thought came to her of her loading the washing machine in the damp basement of her mother's townhouse, the sunlight that would leak through the little window there. She thought of the always-quiet house, the rooms that smelled of stale perfume and cigarette smoke, the closets that reeked of mothballs, the gas stove whose hood stank of too many pan-fried dinners, the creaky floorboards in the upstairs hallway, the loose tiles in the bathroom, the rust stains in the stink. She thought of all this, how it would tower above her, the weight of too many years in one place, and she imagined that if she were loading a washer full of whites, she would pause now to stare at the motes of dust drifting up through the window light, pause and imagine that what she saw was really angel's breath or the lazy rain of Mr. Sandman's stardust—the kind of dreamy nonsense she had imagined as a girl, lying restlessly in her bed while her mother, kneeling close by, whispered fairy tales in her ear to make her sleep.

"And you," she heard the young man saying, "do you like Casual?"

His question, his interest, startled her. She said, "I'll be assistant manager soon." She felt her face flush. She hadn't meant to brag.

"Good for you," he said.

She smiled a little. "I guess you could say I'm ambitious," she said.

"Nothing wrong with that," her young man said. He stood up, wiping a napkin quickly across his lips. The table was a mess. He said, "That was my dinner."

She said, "You don't eat that every night, do you?"

He shrugged. "You going?" he asked.

"No," she said, surprising herself, "I've got some time left." She heard the carolers singing "Here Comes Santa Claus." They sounded like children, almost giddy, though she knew there were no children in the mall's choir.

The young man nodded his goodbye. It looked as if he were about to say something. But he only smiled politely. Then he was gone.

She watched him walk away, a handsome man, better dressed than most. Like someone from a catalogue. The mall now looked more crowded than it had all week. So many people! So much to buy! For the next few minutes she had remaining to herself, she would pretend that she was one of them, the lucky ones, the shoppers. After all, to look at her sitting there, at a messy table, the chair pulled out where the young man had been sitting, who would not imagine that her lover or her husband had left only just now to fetch her something grand?

You're a Sergeant

"When this is over," Captain was saying, "we're going to live in luxury apartments on the Avenue of the Saints, have free cable—eighty-two channels—and everybody's going to shop groceries from their home terminals. We won't ever have to go outside again, we'll live like queen bees!"

I expected Captain to take a bullet in the neck for a stupid statement like that. He was standing on the roof, waving his arms at the cloud-clotted sky, which looked like a gutted mattress—he was an easy target for snipers, a good clean shot right through the neck, but he went on talking, waving those lanky arms, saying anything to goose and gander us. Captain was the oldest of us, nineteen, with a fine mustache thick as his thumb and dyed bright blue, like the color of those downy chicks we used to get for Easter. Lordy, what we'd've given for chicks right now. Some of the guys had been trying to catch pigeons but, stupid as they are, pigeons are surprisingly hard to catch—you get close to them, think you've got them, little waddling squabs within hands-reach, then, Shazamm! (as my Poppi used to say) they're gone, fluttering a little further off. Made me want to shoot one the way Crazy Petre had last week, but you shoot one, we learned, and nothing's left. Hunger makes you stupid, I decided.

Which accounted for Captain's speech, why he'd brought us up to the roof when we should've been below raking through the debris for survivors and stragglers. We've got the Presidential Militia on the run, he said, got 'em scared. We're like pestilence, he said, we're like the wrath of God, we're like the great steel hand of Tetsujin 28! He meant the mighty cartoon robot we boys used to watch on TV. Tetsujin was as tall as a high-rise and could fly, and he was a lovely blue color like our Squad, which was probably why Captain mentioned him. I wished he hadn't because it got me thinking of my brothers and sisters who used to sprawl alongside me while watching TV, so many of them I felt like I was floating in a pool of children. Thirteen brothers and sisters, all still alive and with my mother, I was hoping, on the west side, where the small-electronics corridor was, not a bad part of town, my father and mother refurbishers of PCs and other gear, the apartment crowded with terminal heads and broken glass and wires, which my brothers and sisters couldn't keep their hands away from, busy little hands, tearing through and taking apart any—and everything, curious to know what's inside, what's working, what's this? They were always asking, what's this?

All that activity at home, all those kids, it had been a relief to get away, I had to admit, but now, after eight months in the field, relief meant something very different.

We were listening to Captain do his Captain speech, like I said, all of us gathered on the roof, in plain sight of snipers, when up pops a hand grenade tossed from the street or from a nearby building: it rolls like a warped tennis ball to Captain's duct-taped foot—the grenade looks Russian-made, the casing a nice shiny handful of green pot-metal. Captain glances down at it, blinking his kind fatherly eyes, he's got maybe five seconds before he's blown to bits. "Helluva nice throw, don't you think?" he says, the way he might have complimented a teammate, then he kicks the grenade off the roof and it soars (he was a semi-professional footballer before the war). The rest of us collapse in a panic, folding into the fetal-tuck they taught us in basic training, grip your knees to your chin and wait for the blast. Which doesn't come.

Life is full of surprises, my Poppi often said.

Like me, Poppi was in the Revolutionary Militia too, but somewhere on the frontier, which we'd heard was a horror. It was so bad Captain wouldn't tell me everything he'd heard because he didn't want me to worry, though I worried plenty. We've got to keep our eye on the sparrow, he'd sing to us when we were depressed, keep your eye... dancing around, chucking us under the chin, wagging his finger at us like he was our old man. My own old man was no fighter, too kind, too easy. Every night he'd turn on a couple of PC monitors in the front room, where he and Mama work-shopped their equipment, and we'd gather at his feet in the blue-green light to hear him tell stories, some scary, some funny, his voice like warm water running over us. My thir-teen brothers and sisters would fall asleep before he was finished, then Mama, Poppi and I would carry them up to their pallets, one after the other, precious cargo, little grem-lins, their tiny hands still at last, their pony breaths galloping through cartoon dreams which I would wish for every night I was in the RM.

Captain led us down the bombed-out stairwell. We were strung at careful intervals, automatics ready. We had to be real careful where we stepped, because none of us had boots. When the Revolutionary Militia Recruiters had come to our school nearly a year ago, to sign up everybody over fourteen, they were the handsomest people I'd ever seen, with their shiny automatic rifles and their newly cut bright-blue fatigues with silver buttons and sky-blue berets. Nice haircuts too, some colored in checks of red and yellow, the RM flag. And knee-high leather boots with a shine like the Presidential Fountain at high noon. Oh, yeah, I wanted to look like that. Later, after being painted, tattooed, and finger-printed, I felt stupid when I learned I'd have to wear a pot for a helmet and, instead of a jacket, a bright blue sweatshirt whose dye came off on me when I sweat (and I was sweat-ing a lot, you could be sure). For shoes, they taught us how to construct a shiny silver kind of sandal using duct tape and cutouts from plastic milk cartons. They made a rain-puddle splashing noise whenever we were trotting across asphalt or concrete. Slip-slap. Slip-slap.

But the RM is winning! Captain insisted.

He'd wink and tap a thin finger at his temple as if our brainpower had made the difference, the way we improvise, he said, the way we pulled Crazy Petre out of a storm drain two days ago by tying our rifles together to make a ladder ... we're brilliant, he said, we're a scintillating tide of gray matter, he said, the country's last hope, the glorious sunrise of the future!

We were winning because the Presidential Militia was divided by greed. You didn't need smarts to see that much, everybody in the PM trying to run off with a piece of the President's treasure, his fleet of fifty-six, late-model Ford Tauruses, his pack of pedigree Shih Tzus, his leather furniture, his leather suits, his leather paintings, his collection of glass snow globes, the largest in the world, his six vintage Sherman tanks, his four half-tracks, each with its own wet bar, his touchy land-mine collection, his mint coinage, tons of it, every coin in his image, his Gregory Peckish profile, not to mention his Gregory Peck film archive, the actor he adored most and wanted to emulate, someone tall and righteous like Atticus Finch in *To Kill A Mockingbird*, which the President remade as TKM II, starring the President Himself, with new dialogue He wrote Himself—we children were required to memorize all of his lines by the time we were ten.

"A man is not a bird, though he may fly with brilliant plumage!"

Stuff like that.

The Man, he made us call him. Who's The Man? our teachers would drill us. He's The Man! we would answer in a shout, pointing to his portrait, which was as big as the blackboard. Though we could hardly afford it, each of us boys wore a foulard tied at the neck in a four-in-hand knot just like The Man's, only ours were synthetic, not silk, and the girls had to wear dirndl skirts like His Wife, Trudi, who had made a campaign of Free Movement For Girls, which meant none of them could wear long pants of any kind, much less blue jeans. On special occasions we boys had to paint or polish our shoes white, like The Man's, and the girls had to paint or polish theirs red, like Trudi's. But we children didn't think anything of these demands one way or the other, we had lived so long with so many rules.

Out of the building at last, we and Captain were surprised to find ourselves staring gunpoint to gunpoint at a squad of women-girls, most of their kilts and rags dyed yellow, their faces blackened by the soot of recent fallout or fire. Behind them, you could see where they'd come from, some fighting in the distance, smoke streaming skyward in blue-blackish bands—everyone was convinced all the fires we'd started would blanket the sky with smoke for decades to come, bringing on the new ice age or global warming, nobody could agree which.

We didn't know if the women-girls, were RMs or PMs, because who could you trust? Nobody was what they seemed.

Take one step closer and we open fire, Captain announced calmly. He looked heroic standing there, tall and starving, squinting because he was nearsighted, a nice blue ceramic pot on his head, those long arms gangling out of his too-small sweatshirt, his chapped hands gripping the butt and barrel of his automatic.

Without a thought, my finger was on my trigger, ready to squeeze. I was staring at a woman-girl whose eyes were as blue as Captain's mustache, a scar across the bridge of her nose, maybe a childhood accident like a bike spill, maybe a recent wound. She had almost no eyebrows, she was so fair, one of those milky girls I'd see, the smart ones, at the front of the class, their mouths full of answers, their fingers ever ready to write.

She offered me no more expression than I offered her, though I wanted to smile and would've been happy to make smalltalk. It'd been so long since I'd had a chance to sit with anybody but my six Squad-mates, who were stupid from hunger and itchy with body lice and besides, I'd heard much from them already. I knew everything they would ever say, every complaint about the coppery taste of bad water, about mildewed newsprint for toilet paper, about maddening leg rashes from peeling duct tape....

My name's Lofe, I was ready to blurt. I tried to recall the girls I had liked in school, their faces like pale balloons bobbing in the near-distance, vague girlish forms, their thin arms, their curls (they all had curls in those days), their smiles hidden by their hands, the teasing I relished, the notes I longed for. My name is Lofe!

There were about eight or ten of the women-girls, and they looked well-fed and nowhere near as edgy as I felt.

The leader, who I couldn't see because I was staring at the milky girl, said finally, We're RM Orange Squad.

Looks more like yellow to me, Captain said in a wise-ass way that sounded both playful and threatening.

We're faded, the leader answered.

Doesn't that say it all? I said to myself. *Aren't we all faded?*

Thoughts like this startled me sometimes, made me wonder at how grown up I'd become and scared me because I didn't know what I might say to myself.

Join us for some pigeon, Crazy Petre said (didn't matter to him that there were no pigeons in sight).

No thanks, the orange leader said, we've already eaten.

Lucky! I was thinking.

I saw that the leader was wearing an American football helmet with a ram's design on it and shoulder pads, a sari-wrap of yellow fabric, maybe a curtain, to her knees, and thick-soled hiking boots.

Such shoes! Had she killed somebody to get them?

Again I looked at the Milky One, wanting to kiss her dirty mouth, to smell her unwashed hair, to feel the heat of her face against my hand the way I'd reach for warmth when we gathered around a small flame of rags and scrap some nights, too wasted to worry about drawing fire from snipers. Winter was coming. Yesterday I'd seen snow flurries.

What did the Orange Squad do? I wondered. Our

Squad's specialty was clearance; nobody was supposed to occupy a damaged building. So we chased lots of people into the streets and the stubborn ones we shot, usually in the foot.

Quickly the women-girls moved on. I watched their pale muscled legs, the bulge of their dirty calves, the fine animal sway of their backsides, and I felt like an animal myself. What was becoming of me? A few of the women-girls glanced back to check on us, rifles aimed this way. Look back, I was thinking to the Milky One and, surprise, she did. I gave a little wave, which she didn't return. All business.

Later, walking through the rubble heaps of ruined office towers and thinking again and again of my Milky One, those startled eyes, that scar across her nose, how I wanted to touch it, how I wanted to see her smile, bask in the light of those milk-strong teeth, I announced, I'm in love.

None of my Squad-mates responded, though I was sure they heard and maybe they were thinking the same thing: love.

That was the moment the rubble erupted all around us, geysers of concrete shard and rock dust, pebbles and dirt. I heard us yelping like trapped dogs, ducking into half-standing archways and beneath ledges of overturned walls. Mortars were dropping all around us at a distance of fifty meters and closing. We'd been spotted.

Captain continued standing, took careful aim with his automatic, then opened fire: blam! blam! blam! just like in the comics I used to read by the light of the TV screen. Captain Fury! Captain Nomad! Captain Kingston!

Blam! blam! blam!, the recoil kicking at his shoulder, a gray wisp of smoke leaking from the muzzle, deafening round after deafening round, bullets the size of monster hornets, terrible death-eating bullets, capable of tearing through tank walls, blam! blam! blam!, until his clip was empty and he kneeled to pull out another, at which point a white streak arrowed over him, just missing his head: a rocket! Then we heard the impact, the rocket hitting a brick wall twenty meters behind him, exploding with a force that flattened all of us and sent Captain flying forward like a high-jumper somersaulting over the pole, hands out, his pot-helmet knocked off, his wild blue hair waving like a kerchief.

He's dead, I was thinking, he's gone.

But when we got to him, he wasn't doing badly, his back shredded and pulpy from shrapnel, but otherwise he was whole and conscious, cursing lots and telling us to make a litter so we could carry him away, though we had no idea what a litter was. A *litter*, he explained, something to *carry me away*. Sure, that sounded good to us, but then we wondered aloud where we might carry him. We were so far from Home Base, clear on the other side of the city, a good three days of fighting and dodging to get to.

You better not let me die! he was saying like a threat.

We hustled him away, each of us holding an arm or leg, and he was screaming, Go easy! easy! while the others fired their rifles at random, this way and that, a waste of ammo, but it made a dramatic show for whoever was watching. The mortars had stopped, probably because the enemy had run out or something had jammed or maybe Captain had actually shot a few of them, who could tell?

We found a door that had been split down the middle; surprising it hadn't been taken for firewood, I thought, but then discovered it was plastic. It served well enough as a stretcher for Captain, who we laid facedown on the thing. He was moaning and cursing, opening his eyes now and then to remind us that he was okay. "I'm going to be just fine," he said, and it was then that I realized he was going to die—we couldn't stop his bleeding and he was getting a dopey-sleepy look. He didn't seem in pain, though I suppose he was in greater pain than he knew.

I'd seen plenty of people die already. It wasn't like I wasn't prepared, but this was Captain, and the thought of being without him scared me, like the way I'd been scared after I lost Mama and Poppi in Capital Wal-Mart when I was five, those white-tiled aisles as long as life itself: I'll never get out of there, I thought, I'll never be found, I'll have to sleep on a dog mat in the pet supply department and live on cheese and crackers and candy from the sundries aisle... .

That night, while we hid in an empty automobile

showroom where the shattered glass gleamed on the tile floor like ice just before the river freezes, we argued over what to do with Captain's body. He admitted finally that he was dying. Half-conscious, he kept saying, Don't you leave me for the dogs, don't you *dare* leave me! Stray dogs were eating whatever they could find, and we could hardly blame them. We knew what hunger was. What to do with Captain once he died was a problem, because there wasn't any ground we could get at. We were in the middle of the city, not a clear space to be found for miles, everything buried under many meters of debris, which would be excavated and removed once the war was over, as we hoped it'd be over soon, maybe not this year but next. Even the parks were fortified or land-mined, so you had to be crazy to go near them. Somebody suggested cremation, but none of us had the stomach for it. That's when I said, We'll drop him into the river. Captain perked up at this. I like the water, he said. But he'll float, Duane said, and wash up onto the bank where the dogs'll get him for sure. Or the fish and eels'll get him, said Crazy Petre.

Not if we put him a coffin, I said.

The others laughed. Where are we going to find a coffin?

I remembered seeing a burned-out Minotaur just down street—that would serve nicely, I said, and everybody gasped at the brilliance of my idea. Minotaurs were dreadful three-cylinder cars The Man had invented before he became President. Nearly everybody had one. It didn't matter that every Minotaur ever made was a mechanical failure. Even the new ones needed repairs. You couldn't drive fifty miles without something going wrong. But they were so cheap to buy and cheap to fix, even if it was a terrible inconvenience, everybody kept buying them, which made a millionaire out of The Man, who named the Minotaur *The Car of The Nation* once he became President.

Poppi said the Minotaur looked like a crumpled felt hat, it was a national disgrace, the Minotaur tire hardly bigger than a wheel of cheese and the seats simply plastic-wrapped aluminum webbing. The one we found down the street was without wheels and completely gutted, the front and back windows shattered but intact. We figured they'd hold. The side windows we duct-taped over, then we set Captain inside—he was mumbling, Thank you, thank you. We slammed the doors and hefted the whole thing onto our shoulders like one of those fancy sedan chairs rich folk were carried around in centuries ago.

We hadn't walked two blocks when Captain started rapping at the floorboard like he had something urgent to say, so we eased the Minotaur down, opened the door, and peeked in. He looked kind of shriveled from the loss of blood and terribly dejected. I imagined it was terribly lonely lying in there.

Captain pointed a trembling finger at me and said, You're a sergeant, Lofe! You're a sergeant!

Then he lay back, folded his hands neatly at his waist, and he was dead. Nobody had to touch or inspect him to see that much.

The others looked at me like my ears were on fire.

I'm a sergeant!, I was thinking, promoted! And I wondered if I'd have the nerve to stand the way Captain had and shoot into the empty distance, if I could grow a mustache as fine as his, if my men, all of them younger than I was, would follow me anywhere the way we had followed Captain.

As we carried Captain's Minotaur to the river, under cover of darkness, walking hastily down Amanda Perez Boulevard, controversially named after one of Trudi's pet snakes, we saw pink flares light up the cloud billow to the west now and then—they looked like shooting stars. I told the Squad that traditionally in literature the west represents death, because that's where the sun sets. I heard my men-boys mutter their approval because already I was taking control, showing off my knowledge, though really I felt foolish because I was thinking, could I somehow sew three stripes to my sweatshirt? Would the Milky woman-girl be impressed if she knew I'm a sergeant? Thinking things like this while carrying Captain in that little car on our shoulders, the man not dead ten minutes. How callous can you get?

It felt colder by the river, and I thought I saw fist-sized chunks of ice floating by in the black current, which looked fast, but maybe everything looks faster in the dark, I was thinking. The trees were gone, cut for firewood, and the bank was littered on both side with crushed brick, overturned asphalt, rusted pipes, and boulders as big as TV sets—so many boulders like they'd fallen from the sky. Who put them there? It wasn't easy getting down to the water. Watch your step, I cautioned everyone, easy, easy! I said, then I remembered this was what Captain had said as we carried him away earlier. That's when I felt my eyes stinging. It seemed to me I was burying my own Poppi, and I began to think that I'd never see him again.

We slid the Minotaur into the water and the river seemed to eat it hungrily, the little car dropping so quickly into the blackness, snow flurries swirling over the eddies it made, and we all stared at what was gone. I was thinking how years from now I'd look into the river and picture our Captain down there, long buried by mud and silt, like a strange time capsule. I promised myself I'd never forget and I'd try to visit him when I could, maybe throw flowers into the water and say a little prayer if I could remember one. I probably couldn't since even now, as we stared at the black water, snow flurries as big as bottle caps tumbling over us, the start of a heavy snow, flares blinking in the clouds behind us, I couldn't think of a single holy thing to say.

Telephone:
an Act in Three Plays

On a Thursday morning, while I was working at home, and the fringe of a hurricane was hurtling itself at the windows of my apartment and all of Baltimore, my ex-wife phoned to tell my that our former therapist had just been arrested for child molestation. Sexual assault, third-degree: touching the girl's genitals. "Oh, God!" I kept saying. "Oh, no!" I really liked the man, had been seeing him up until a few months previously because I wasn't faring as well as I thought I should have been, at least not as well as my ex-wife. "I just thought you'd want to know," she said, "because I know you don't read the paper." A reporter, she scours the paper every day. I myself don't like bad news. Isn't it enough that I'm aware of the world's evil? Must I be reminded every day?

It occurred to me that this was an overture of sorts. I could hear her shortness of breath. Was she upset at the news or was she anxious about talking with me? Or maybe it was the storm. She hates storms. We hadn't spoken in ten months, not since last October, after the divorce was final and we'd run into each other at the Y. Actually, she knew my schedule and had sought me out, laying some mail at my feet like an offering and then running from the gym as I pursued her. In tears, both of us. That night we slept together, after some exhaustive love-making. There was still plenty of love left, at least on my part, though she made clear her motivation had as much to do with sympathy—dare I say *pity*?—as it had to do with love. The divorce had been her idea. "It's not too late," I told her at the breakfast table. We were eating multigrain cereal and blueberries, with lactose-free milk (she has IBS). Her silence, her pensive mastication, her forlorn gaze into her breakfast bowl were answer enough. On my way out, I said, "Don't do this again." And for a time, at least a day, I felt stronger, determined to start anew, never mind I had just turned forty-three, as awkward an age, it seems, as twenty-three.

Her call, after these many months, exhilarated me and dismayed me all at once—I was exhilarated by the surprise, exhilarated too by the bad news, by the fact that *I* wasn't the one who had been arrested, who perhaps had ruined his own (and another's) life; and I was dismayed for the same reasons but, above all, because hearing her voice again exhilarated me. The way a former smoker would be exhilarated after taking a deep drag of the forbidden weed and knowing in that heady instance that he was lost again to his addiction. Although Steffi was no addiction, there was something *pathological* in my attraction to her, especially after all she'd put me through. Henry, our former therapist, had helped me see this much.

"I suppose I should call him," I said at last.

"He *molested a child,* Douglas."

"We don't know that for certain," I answered. "Maybe he needs a friend."

"Healthy people don't befriend their analysts."

"Therapist is different from analyst, I think."

You can see how it was with us. I felt the conversation give way as abruptly as a dry-rotted floorboard. And soon we were arguing, even though I knew, as Steffi must have known, that it was silly to act this way.

Later, depressed again, staring out at the willows that were bowed in the wind, blunt bullets of rain thumping at my windows, I remembered that this storm had been named Henry. And I wondered what my former therapist might be thinking, released on bail, locked in his modest split-level with his two chocolate labs while Hank railed at the world.

The urge to phone him grew immense.

I didn't phone him simply because my ex-wife said I shouldn't; nor did I phone him because I pitied the man. I phoned him because I was convinced that if he answered his phone, if he were willing to take that risk right now, he would be a better man for it. And somehow so would I.

I

However, sadly, when I picked up the phone again, the line was dead. Irony of ironies! How disconcerting it was to press my hot ear to that cool plastic and receive— nothing. The kind of silence I imagined might engulf a mime's nightmare. Like total darkness. It was so unnerving that I shook the receiver as if to loosen something and make it deliver. The world should *deliver*, I thought, some things *must* hold, must be predictable. It seemed then and it seems now that this moment should have yielded a lesson of some magnitude but, to this day, well after my ex-wife has married a very successful roofing contractor and long after my therapist was released on bail and later disappeared, some say to Argentina, to this day I couldn't tell you what that lesson might have been.

II

I dialed, my fingers trembling—I missed the buttons twice—then I waited two rings, four rings. Nothing. Not even his answering machine. I tried later and it was the same: he did not answer. Not that day, nor the next, nor the next. But how could I judge what this meant? Maybe he'd gone out of town; maybe he was staying with a friend; maybe he's smarter than I and knows that a wise man keeps silent when others look upon him with distaste and distrust. In any case, I never heard what became of him—I didn't want to know and I refused to let Steffi tell me in her breathless way, even though she tried twice. Both times I hung up on her, and since then I have screened my calls. To her credit, I must admit, she could have dropped the info on my machine, but she spared me. And, in this, I wonder if she knows how much love she has shown me.

III

When he answered, he sounded the same as ever, the dogs barking behind him: "Oh, hi, Doug—quiet, Mindy; quiet, Miranda!" Then he said, "You feeling okay? You want to get together and talk?"

"I'm okay," I said, though I knew I sounded depressed. "What about you?"

"Same as usual," he said. I pictured him shrugging. "Still collecting antique toys." His house was full of them. Tin, mostly.

"I just wanted to say hi, let you know I was thinking of you," I said.

"That's nice," he said. "That's nice of you. Call me if you need to talk."

"I'll do that," I said. "Thanks."

Then he hung up and, more than ever, I had an urge to see Steffi. As if she would right my world, which seemed to be tipping like a capsized iceberg.

How could Henry be so *normal* on the phone? I wanted to ask her.

When Steffi picked up and heard my voice again (it really felt like I had phoned her first—but she had phoned me, hadn't she?), I heard her sigh, as if to say, You're so predictable.

She said, "You called him, didn't you?"

"I called him." Then I waited, baiting her because I knew she was no better than I; she had to hear more.

"He never picks up his phone," she insisted.

"He did this time."

She waited a beat, then blurted, "And...?"

"And he was very normal, Steff. Like it was another day."

"What did you expect?"

"I expected he'd sound hurt or depressed."

"It's *you* who sounds depressed."

Now I sighed. "Maybe we should have dinner."

"I'm not going out in this weather."

"Otherwise you would go out with me, is that what you're saying?"

She was quiet for a moment. I pictured her leaning back in her rocker, where she reads, and gazing at the ceiling, something she always did when she had to think hard.

"Douglas, what are you trying to do?"

"You know what I'm trying to do."

"Stop it."

"You're the one who called me, don't forget."

"I thought you'd want to know."

"Thanks," I said. "Now I know. My therapist is bound for prison."

"The world's not a pretty place," she said. As if I needed reminding.

"Is that your project, proving that the world is not a pretty place?"

"Let's not do this, Douglas. I've got to go."

I glanced behind me, the darkened apartment yawning like a cave. I thought, *I need a cat*. Then, as calmly as I could manage, I said, "You're right, Steff, you've got to go."

Then I hung up.

Later, as I sat at the window and watched the storm, I was thinking how that last line was like something from a movie, the kind of thing the tough guy says to the babe he leaves behind. But then, as I considered my therapist and what awaited him and my ex-wife and how she lived, scanning the papers for disasters, I decided that being a tough guy, even if I could manage it, would neither be satisfying nor sufficient, not if you choose, like I have, to live in a world like this.

Red Shoes

By the time I got through the forest, the revolution was over and the President, his wife, and his lieutenant were swinging by their necks from the lion-faced gargoyles of the cathedral. The people stoned the corpses, which looked like gargoyles themselves, hardly human. I recalled seeing something like it in an old newsreel: Mussolini, dead and bloated, hanging upside-down from the balcony of his apartment and wearing only a T-shirt and trousers, his people throwing stones. So much hate.

From where I was standing, I could not see much. Not that I wanted to. Three pendulums swaying slowly from high up the cathedral, the endless tolling of bells. The ocean roar of people. It did not seem real, any of it, the end of war, the end of tyranny. What did I know of our dead President—The Man, he called himself—except that the money he printed was no good (I used it to paper my children's tattered books) and that his promises were as empty as the shells of gutted television sets that now lined the Avenue of the Beloved Saints? But, oh, how The Man could stir our passions when he spoke! And he had a triumphant smile; he seemed to know so much more than we knew.

When the fighting grew intense and the capital was besieged, I knew I would have to join the Revolutionary

Militia. It was for me literally a matter of life and death. The RM would have found me in my shop, cobbling computers from scavenged parts—business was quite good, really, until the siege—and they would have charged me with indifferent collaboration. "Doing nothing is doing something" was one of the RM's slogans.

Frankly, I was happy to leave my fourteen children. Living with them was like living with barely-tamed animals. In jest, Sofi and I often vowed never to touch one another again. "Look what becomes of love," I would say, gesturing to the children. Everywhere there were children. Children pulling pages from our precious books, children picking plaster from our apartment walls, children gouging our dining table with their breakfast spoons, children peeling tiles from our kitchen floor, children wrenching knobs from our doors and faucet handles from our sink, children unscrewing bulbs from lights and, inevitably, dropping them, bombs of delicate glass. It was all Sofi and I could do to feed them and, at the same time, keep our business going.

Because of migraines, terrible hatchet-bladed pain hammering at my eyes, the RM made me a dispatcher. I wore a pot for a helmet, we were so desperate for supplies. I carried a colonial-era musket which took four minutes and thirty-three seconds to load, and I had to be careful of the barrel overheating, maybe the chamber exploding in my face. That had happened to another dispatcher, who lost an eye and half his nose.

When word of our victory came, I was crouched naked in a plastic tub, ankle-deep in Malathion, trying to delouse myself. There was no easy return to the capital, since all of the roads were mined. As we made our way through the forest, we heard the pop-pop of mines exploding in the distance, each one marking certain death or maiming.

Pushing through the crowds in the capital was as difficult as pushing through the forest thickets. I was angry at their obstruction, the way the oblivious mob clotted the streets and alleys—I had to get home. I had been away for nearly two years and I feared that, in the last months of fighting, Sofi and the children had been forced to join the RM. Or worse. Though I believe in no God, I had prayed every night for a dreamless sleep.

RM soldiers were giving out gifts to everyone who had helped in the fighting. "Don't you want your gift?" someone was shouting at me. I was struggling to walk in the opposite direction but the crowd was nearly impassable. The stranger, a captain with log-thick arms, grabbed me by the shoulder of my coat and turned me around. "You deserve a gift—get in line, my friend." Son of a bitch, I was tempted to butt him with my musket. But he had a new automatic slung from his shoulder and another in his belt.

While we waited in line, the defeated soldiers of the Presidential Militia served us bowls of cold rice and chocolate kisses. With edgy enthusiasm, they repeated, "The Man is dead!" We nodded in return and said, "He sure is!" The chocolate made me giddy. When the guns went off, I fired mine too. My ears were ringing. I thought I might faint. Then, at last, I was at the palace doors, where the RM soldiers were distributing booty. But all they had left were shoes, heaps of ladies' shoes—hundreds, perhaps thousands, of them—which had belonged to the President's wife.

I got a pair of red satin slippers with leather soles and red silk laces. The laces had once been adorned with gold tassels. The tassels I did not know about until I was walking away and someone said, "Those used to have gold tassels, right here, I seen them on TV."

"These?" I said. "Really?"

"You been cheated, friend. Where's the gold?"

I shrugged.

He offered a bitter smile. "You said it, friend. There ain't no gold."

Something is better than nothing, I was tempted to tell him but it occurred to me that this might have been another RM slogan and not a thought I would have voiced myself.

I rushed away and was relieved when the crowds

thinned. I was never alone, however, because people were living in the streets. Many had set up house in abandoned trams and automobiles. Some were constructing lean-tos of desktops and room-dividers from office buildings. In many parts, the capital was still smoldering, and it was not unusual to come upon a body now and then. My great fear was that I would see someone I knew sprawled in the rubble, even one of my own children. I saw a dog sniffing at a body, maybe a young woman, near the ruined library and I raised my musket to scare him off, but when I pulled the trigger, nothing happened. I had forgotten to reload.

As soon as I entered my own street, I heard loud-speaker music booming from a rooftop nearby. It sounded like "Fly Me to The Moon." The street itself was bathed in pools of lovely white-blue light, which spilled from three half-ruined big-screen TVs, their pictures scrambled with snowy static. It was a good sign, I thought, that there was electricity. The buildings had a fairy-tale appearance, their fractured roofs looking crenelated, like ancient castles, their windows gouged open in fanciful patterns. In a clearing on the asphalt, amid the heaps of rubble, several couples were ballroom dancing, a few of them haltingly, probably drunk. The women needed more partners, I could see immediately, and a few beckoned me. There was Masha, Niki, Ludi, Seraf. They hardly recognized me. Had I changed so much?

"You're so thin!" they said, patting me on the back, pinching my bony cheeks. They looked none too good themselves, dough-faced, sunken-eyed. But under their scrutiny I felt terribly self-conscious, ugly and ill, like a terminal cancer patient released for his last visit home.

"My wife?" I croaked, fighting back the tears. "My children?"

"Fine! Down there. Go! Look. Fine!" They waved me on, and I was not two steps away when they commenced dancing again.

There was nothing left of our apartment, but the children were still breaking and picking at what they could.

Sofi had put them to work gathering brick, lathe, and plaster. When she saw me, she brought herself up, arms folded over her chest, and said, "Where have *you* been?" as if I had simply missed dinner. She looked the same, a little thicker, her eyes red from a lack of sleep, her lips chapped and bitten from worry. She wore a man's pinstriped pants suit and blue rubber Wellingtons. The children nearly carried me to her in a swarm, kissing my knees, my hands, my elbows, my ears. "Poppi!" they cried.

"Miraculous that you're in one piece," Sofi said, examining my hands, kissing my blackened fingers. I thought of the men and women who would return home in aluminum boxes, some no larger than a roasting pan.

Only one child was missing, Lofe, our eldest. He had joined the RM shortly after I had. "Time for him to come back," I said.

"He wants a career," Sofi said.

"There's no career in the RM," I said.

"He's a sergeant," she said.

"He's sixteen years old!"

"Still," she said. "They needed men."

"Boys, you mean."

She shrugged, pretending that it couldn't be helped, though I could tell it pained her greatly, the way her eyes skidded to the ruined building tops, to the darkened sky.

"If we act fast," she said, brightening, "we could loot some buildings, maybe get enough processors for six months' work."

The children hurrahed at this. "Loot, loot, loot!" they crowed.

"We'll all be killed," I said.

"One way or another," Sofi said.

"Let's sell these shoes." I held them over the children's heads. They jumped for them; they would have torn them to shreds in minutes.

"Where are the gold tassels?" Sofi asked, examining one with a surprisingly expert touch.

"Did you see them on TV?" I asked.

"When do I have time to watch TV?"

"The gold tassels are gone," I said.

"Did you sell them?"

"Loot, loot, loot!" the children chanted.

"How can I sell what I don't have?"

Sofi handed back the shoe. "These aren't worth half a week's groceries."

"They're silk," I said.

"Satin," she corrected.

"Loot, loot, loot!" the children sang.

"The RM intermediary government says we'll have work in the new automobile plant."

"Promises," she said. "What do we live on until then?"

"What *have* you been living on?" I asked.

"You don't want to know."

Mice, crickets, roaches, earthworms.

Whatever it was, it tasted good to me. I ate two hubcaps of the stuff, Sofi ladling it out with one of the lady's shoes. The other shoe she used as a mitt to hold the pot, the only one she had not surrendered to the ammunition drive.

"You'll ruin them like that," I said.

She eyed me with mock disdain.

I was thinking that some sloughed-off skin cells of the President's wife resided in that shoe Sofi was using as a ladle, and now I was going to eat them. This was not what the RM meant when it said, "War makes cannibals of us all."

When it was time for bed, we gathered around the small fire of my last book, a collection of monk songs, which the family had saved for my return. It made an intense, blue-flamed heat. We held our open hands to it as if begging for a tram token. At the children's request, I told a story about a returning soldier who ate from the shoe of the dead President's wife; some of her sloughed-off skin cells in the shoe clung to his food and after eating them, he felt better than he had a right to feel. In fact, he felt like buying everything he could buy, clothes mostly, but also silver pots and brass-bottomed pans and marble beads and pickled peacock feet. He grew so terribly extravagant that he exceeded the limits of his fourteen credit cards and was soon jailed for failure to pay his bills.

This made the children cry and complain, "Don't go to jail!" as if I had the power to stop such a thing.

"I'm not done!" I told them.

From his fourteen credit cards, which the police had thrown out the window of his house and into a neighbor's compost heap, sprang fourteen children ranging in ages from four to sixteen. His children lived on dirt, in fact loved to eat dirt, and so it was no trouble for them to eat the dirt below the city jail. Thus they freed their father. Then they ate a trough to the sea, which soon filled with water and became the longest river in the country. Then they all swam away to other countries, though they never stayed in one place for long because the children always ate it up.

My family applauded the end of my story, and I was grateful because I knew it wasn't very good. I was out of practice, after all. As the children nodded off, huddled one against the other, backsides and thighs as pillows, Sofi and I eyed each other with longing. I heard the firecracker sound of distant gunfire, either celebrations or snipers, then more loudspeaker music, this time from far off. Violins, it sounded like.

The next morning, on our way to loot a high-rise made of pink glass and black girders, we saw Lofe and two other young RM Officers hanging upside down from a hotel portico. At first I thought they were dead—I was about to tear out my thinning hair and wail in grief—but then I saw that they were simply exercising, hanging from the exposed pipes by the crook of their knees and swinging childishly, their automatic rifles gripped in both hands. They aimed at us when we approached, I in the lead.

"War's over, Lofe, time to come home," I said.

He lowered his rifle and grinned at me. "Pop," he said. "You look like hell."

"I feel better than that," I said. "It's good to see you."

Lofe had grown tall since I'd left, taller than I, it appeared. He had a downy brown mustache and his hair was enviably long. A pretty boy, I thought. His mother's looks, those long lashes, that fine complexion. I wanted to kiss him but this would have embarrassed him, I knew. His wrinkled uniform needed cleaning, a jam stain on the right shoulder as large as an ashtray.

"I'm on patrol," he said. "Can't budge."

"What's there to patrol?" I said.

"Have to watch for looters," he said. "These are desperate times." He aimed his rifle at an imaginary target in the distance. A pedestrian across the street shouted, "Don't you *dare* shoot me!"

"Desperate measures for desperate times" was another RM slogan, this one invented to rationalize the induction of children into the infantry.

"You're looking at a family of looters," I said, at which the children began chanting, "Loot, loot, loot!" Sofi shushed them.

"An unfortunate turn of events," Lofe said. "I have to arrest you, do you know that?"

"You can't arrest us for something we haven't done yet," I said.

"Right," he said. He sounded relieved.

"Why don't you come down from there and follow us to a looting," I said. "Then you can arrest us in the act."

"Of course," he said. He got down. His comrades remained dangling. "I'll be back shortly," he told them.

In near-unison, they said, "Later, Lofe."

I felt bad that Lofe was so dimwitted, but what can you expect of a boy who had been carrying a rifle around for two years? I could only imagine, and tried not to, the damage he had done to others and to himself.

"You think they'll have enough room in the prisons for all of us?" Sofi asked, goading him. I had heard that the prisons were overcrowded with enemies of the revolution.

"We'll make room," he said.

This was another RM slogan: "We'll make what we need when we need it."

"What did you get for fighting?" he asked me. "That silly musket?" I was still carrying the weapon, even though it wasn't loaded.

"These red slippers," I said, nodding to my swollen, slippered feet.

He gave them a cursory glance, then grinned at me. "See my gold tooth?"

"They gave you that?"

"Twenty-four karat," he said proudly.

The children were picking at Lofe's uniform. Already they had removed the silver piping from his shirt and the buttons of his pockets. I was gratified to see how gently he tried to swat them away. War has not ruined him, I told myself.

The children had already taken the laces of my slippers so that now they flapped at my soles. By the time we got to the high-rise, they had stripped Lofe down to his T-shirt and trousers, each child with a ripped fragment of his once-glorious shirt. "You'll make a good father," Sofi told Lofe. He smiled mildly, pretending that it didn't matter. He had to hold his rifle over his head to keep the children from messing with it.

The high-rise had been thoroughly looted already, we discovered. Nothing remained but a few mainframe shells and frayed network lines. We checked every floor, Lofe leading the way, his rifle at ready. I must admit, I felt better with him in the lead.

"Yield to the young!" Another RM slogan.

We looked into several other high-rises but had no luck. The children paraded about with useless plastic scrap clapping pieces together as they marched behind us along the avenue. When I glanced back to check on them I was startled to see that others had joined us—a procession of hopeful citizens, young and old.

Sofi said, "Apparently they think we know where

we're going."

"I fear their disappointment when they realize we're going nowhere," I said.

"We're going somewhere," Lofe asserted. He was scouting the distance: a coil of smoke rising from a church steeple, disabled automobiles down the avenue, pedestrians waving as we approached, some onlookers tossing Styrofoam peanuts at us from office tower windows, the white stuff raining down like confetti.

I envied Lofe for his youthful adamancy, his belief that we'd find something worth stealing in this picked-over city.

Some of those who joined our procession followed the children's example and began clapping together plastic scrap they'd found along the way. The noise was tremendous, like the slap and drum of marching elephants. It was almost frightening. And, like a clamorous spell, it compelled yet more passersby to join us.

Every time we arrived at an abandoned building, our crowd would swarm into it, find nothing of note, then swarm out, bringing with it more recruits for the procession. We marched out of the city and late into the night, pausing to camp briefly in a field of ruined corn, which one of us inadvertently set afire, a orange-glowing spectacle we left at dawn.

At midday, Lofe admitted to me in a whisper, "I don't know where we're going." He sounded boyish now, frightened. He hadn't been vigilant about his rifle and the children had dismantled it: he carried only the skeleton of the thing, a butt and a barrel. I cautioned Sofi to check the children for ammunition; if we weren't careful they'd eat it.

It seemed that our three-kilometer ragtag procession of citizens subsisted only on the noise they made as we marched. Their expectations sustained them. As we neared the coastal flats, a small single-prop plane flew low over us and wagged its wings as if in warning. Would it bomb us? I felt surprisingly protective of these strangers behind me, these gullible hopefuls. I shook my fist at the plane. Behind me I saw others following my example.

When we reached the sea, we found the flowers in bloom. "Don't eat those, they'll make you sick," I cautioned the children, but too late. They and the others denuded the coast of red poppies and yellow mustard blossoms. Even Sofi tried one. "Bitter," she said with a grimace, then she offered me one. I thought of the Land of the Lotus Eaters, how nice it would be if we could forget all we had been through.

After everyone had retched and spit up their flowers, we gathered at the shore and watched the water, which was as calm as a lake, hardly a ripple of waves. With the others—perhaps a thousand or more—behind me, waiting, I felt a tremendous pressure to offer some explanation for what had brought us here. My head was aching, the start of a migraine. Would we swim like lemmings to our death? I wondered.

The crowd was murmuring; several of my children, or maybe they were someone else's children, were still clapping their scrap like an impatient audience.

It occurred to me that some gesture was necessary. So I slipped off my red shoes, which were truly remarkable shoes, I decided, since the soles had not worn through despite our ninety kilometers of walking—my feet were terribly blistered and I wondered how I had escaped the pain— I slipped off the shoes, stepped into the shallows, and the crowd fell silent. Even the children ceased their racket. Gingerly I set the slippers on the water and, lo, they floated, like small red boats. I heard, behind me, everyone muttering their approval and relief, so I waded deeper, as if to exhort or somehow impel the shoes onward. We watched them drift away, side by side; at one point they nudged each other and I feared that they would sink abruptly but, small miracles, they stayed their course. I wanted to believe, I tried to believe as the others did, that the shoes went on floating—and would float forever—because at that moment I lost sight of them, far out in the water, their toes pointed to the horizon, where sunset was pinking the cloudless sky.

the Day His Wife's Face Froze

I

He was teaching art to his sixth graders. They were making papier-mâché masks for Halloween. He was thinking of the turning of leaves, the sunburst colors, the acrid scent of leaf rot and tannin, leaf stains on the sidewalk like paleolithic handprints. One of the boys had just painted both of his hands red with tempera—as though he'd dipped them in a bucket of blood; he was flashing them like spooked bats over the girls' heads.

Some of the girls squealed in delighted fright; others laughed.

He sent the boy to the vice principal.

The boy regarded him with resentment and disbelief as if Teacher had no sense of humor.

He, conscientious teacher, was tempted to say to them all, "What a stupid waste of paint!" but he thought better of it.

Why be a bore?

The boys were making superhero robot faces that looked to him like Kabuki masks. The girls were making cartoon teddy bear faces inspired by the latest fad, the grinning teddy face blazoned on their backpacks, their wristbands, their T-shirts, their water bottles.

The boys had grown silent, grimly intent on their painting. They were fantasizing, no doubt, about destruction wrought by their own superheroic strengths.

The girls were chatting, painting purple bears, blue bears, pink bears. And fantasizing, no doubt, about dancing and magic: their brand of deliverance.

Will this never change? he wondered.

Then the ghostly goggle-eyed vice principal appeared at the window of the classroom door.

A startling sight.

Among the children, he was notorious for his stealthy approach.

Maybe he wanted a word about the painter.

But the VP seemed reluctant to enter and, through the door's window, beckoned with raised brows and a slight nod.

The children watched with feigned disinterest.

Halloween was just a week away.

The VP had bad news—somehow this was clear.

II

When he found his wife at the hospital, she was sitting in a cubicle in the emergency ward. She wore a green smock, her feet were bare. She looked *embarrassed*.

He took her hand, kissed one hot cheek, kneeled beside her, their eyes meeting at last.

"They said you're all right," he began, "but—"

"It's stupid, really," she said.

He was aware of examining her, his eyes running over every limb, like checking his son after a fall.

No blood.

But the absence of visible wrong made the hairs on his arms stand on end, his voice quaver, his fingers tremble as if he himself had just escaped a harrowing accident.

"It's my face," she said. "It stopped working."

He saw it now: half her face—the right side—was frozen. Paralyzed. How odd, how damaged it made her look.

When she attempted a smile, it was as if she were wearing a cruel, mocking mask. Bell's Palsy, the GP guessed, though a neurologist would have to confirm. It could be nothing.

Had she sat in front of an air conditioner lately, received an uncommon chill? Bell's usually subsides in a few days. Or a few weeks. Unless it is the symptom of a tumor.

But that was unlikely.

"Let's hope it holds till Halloween," she said. This time, when she attempted a smile, a loop of saliva slipped over her lower lip.

III

One week and many tests later, it was Halloween and still half her face was frozen. On that side she looked drowsy, doped. She was a good sport about it. Their son, seven, kept saying, "You look *so* weird, Mom."

The doctors had ruled out a brain tumor. Bell's is a mystery, they insisted. The longer she remained frozen, however, the less likely her chance of recovery.

Every night before sleep, she would lay her head in his lap and he would drip saline solution—three drops—into her droopy-lidded eye to keep down the inflammation since she could not close the lid.

And now she made love with a desperate enthusiasm that both exhilarated and scared him. Did she know something he did not?

"We'll get to the bottom of this," he assured her.

"How deep would the bottom be?" she mused.

"Remember what my father used to say to me?"

"No," she said.

"When you hear hoofbeats behind you, what do you expect to see, horses or zebras?" He perceived the start of a smile in her lips.

"Depends where I am," she said.

"You should expect horses, of course."

"Oh, I see."

"Horses," he said again.

Sometimes she wore a patch over her afflicted eye. Their son loved the patch. "Wear it for Halloween!" he begged. She did, with a broad-brimmed hat, a black body stocking, and a black cape that fluttered in the breeze. She needed help negotiating the stairs because, with the use of only one eye, she had poor depth perception.

It was a blustery, cloudless night with a blue wedge of moon, dead leaves scuttering in sidewalk eddies. Nine years previously they had thought of getting married on Halloween but hadn't the patience to wait that long.

As they watched their son—a Ninja Ranger—run from door to door, he said, "We could have another child, don't you think?"

She raised her eye patch to get a better look at him and said, "I didn't know you were that scared."

He was terrified, he realized. He'd had it too easy.

IV

The next year, a week before Halloween, he was teaching another class of sixth graders. They were painting their papier-mâché masks. He had made one too. It was the face of Fate, he decided: inscrutable and half-palsied. The children said it was frightful, though he hadn't intended it to be.

His wife had long since recovered. The doctors could not explain how or why, the Bell's having subsided as mysteriously as it had appeared. He had thought that now—after their brief brush with catastrophe—everything would change for him, that he would enjoy life more fully, be more grateful for every moment with his wife and his son. But now they continued as before.

Sometimes he lost patience with his son, some days he did not want to talk with his wife. Her paralysis seemed no more than a fit of coughing that one soon forgets. Only he had not forgotten.

Hence the mask.

He thought he'd make her a gift of it but then

thought otherwise. What was he trying to prove? Then he tried giving away the mask—which he had painted purple—but none of the children would take it, as if they knew that he had made something too weighty for their little heads. So, at the day's end, he threw it into the school Dumpster.

That night while lying beside his wife, who slept with a soundness he had come to envy, he imagined someone finding the mask and taking it home and wondering, maybe for years to come, What could have possessed the maker to create such a face, that drowsy right side, that odd half-smile?

about Ron Tanner

Before pursuing a writing career, Ron Tanner worked as a musician on the California honky-tonk and Nevada casino circuits. He has also worked as a yard man, a door-to-door salesman, and a customs clearance clerk. Although he is a California native, most of his relatives come from the Carolina hills. He was a James A. Michener fellow at the University of Iowa, where he received his MFA. He also holds a PhD from the University of Wisconsin-Milwaukee. His stories have appeared in such magazines as *The Iowa Review, The Massachusetts Review*, and *The Quarterly*. His awards include a Pushcart Prize, a Maryland State Arts Council grant, the *New Letters* Literary Award, *The Literary Review*'s Charles Angoff Award, and the Faulkner Society Award. He chairs the Communication Department at Loyola College in Baltimore, Maryland. *A Bed of Nails* is his first book. He is now working on a novel about the Marshall Islands.

about Janet Burroway

Janet Burroway selected *A Bed of Nails* for the first G.S. Sharat Chandra Prize. She is the author of seven novels, including *The Buzzards, Raw Silk* (runner up for the National Book award), *Opening Nights*, and *Cutting Stone;* a volume of poetry, *Material Goods;* and two children's books, *The Truck on the Track* and *The Giant Jam Sandwich.* Her award-winning plays have received readings and productions in New York, London, and elsewhere. She is also the author of *Writing Fiction.* She is Robert O. Lawton Distinguished Professor Emeritus at the Florida State University in Tallahassee.